ISBN: 1507531036
ISBN 13: 978-1507531037

Saying thank you to S. Marquis, Mary, Marie, Natasha, my family and friends will never be enough. They helped me tremendously and I am forever grateful to each of you because this book would not have been possible without you. To my dearest daughter, Kaylie, know that one day we will overcome the obstacles before us and, no matter what, Daddy has and forever will love you.

Milton Johnson

Johnson turned on the hot water two minutes ago. It had been running so long that steam had fogged up the lower part of the mirror he was looking into. With his emotions still running high because of the funeral for Vice President Rafael Perez and not thinking about the temperature of the water, he put his hands in the basin to splash some water on his face and immediately pulled them out because the water scalded him. Broken from his trance, Johnson looked in the mirror and gave himself a pep talk. Inhaling deeply, he began speaking to himself with a voice so low only he could hear it.

"They will go only as far as you will take them."

He looked into the sink and stared at his reflection in the water he had let pool there and continued to repeat the phrase.

"They will go only as far as you will take them."

He began to splash the now slightly cooler water on his face to muffle the sound of his voice. He didn't want anyone to hear him talking to himself and think he was going insane because this was a day he needed everyone around him to have complete confidence in every word that will come out of his mouth.

As he lifted his face up from the sink and looked in the mirror, focusing on the water running down his chin, he began to reflect about his father, Roger. He remembered telling his father, as he sat in his favorite chair, that he had won the starting quarterback position on his varsity high school football team. He could tell his dad was so proud of him, but being as macho as he was, Roger would never let Johnson know it.

Instead, his father had given him the advice that made him into the man he was today.

"Success is no coincidence," Roger had said. "Very few men have a vision, and the ones who don't have a vision will need to be led. The few who do, rarely follow through because they lack execution."

Roger had paused midsentence as he had stared into the brandy in his glass, as if the liquid inside was showing him a picture of his life. Once he had broken his self-imposed trance, he had raised the glass to his lips and looked Johnson in the face. "The men with all the talent and no execution create a natural check

PS_BX05415448

CreateSpace
7290 Investment Drive Suite B
North Charleston, SC 29418

Question About Your Order?
Log in to your account at www.createspace.com and "Contact Support."

03/23/2016 03:28:20 PM
Order ID: 122023645

Qty.   Item

IN THIS SHIPMENT

The Weight Of The World
1507531036

and balance for the men out there with less talent and the know-how to execute and implement their visions. These men are willing to take success, even by force if necessary. From now on, Milton, master the behavior of following through, because if you do, success will lay in the bed for you like a woman ready to be taken."

He had paused again and looked at Johnson. "From this day forward, those men will look to you and remember your face for the rest of their lives. Use this day to determine what kind of man you are! Are you one with vision and execution or one with talent and no follow through? Whichever it is, they will see it right away, so be strong, and let your eyes convince them. Now go on and tell your mother this wonderful news."

Johnson had risen out of his seat and hugged his dad, but his dad did not hug him back. Instead, he had felt his father bury his head into his shoulders, and that was all Johnson needed to know he had made him proud.

As he ended his reminiscing and focused on his face in the mirror, Johnson could hear his father's voice. He repeated the words to himself. "Let your eyes convince them…Let your eyes convince them…Let your eyes convince them."

After saying it three times in the mirror, he was ready to face his peers. He opened the bathroom door and saw one of his assistants, Sasha, holding a dozen folders. Each of the folders was stamped with the word "Classified."

"How do I look, Sasha?"

"Like a million dollars."

"Thank you, my sweet. Don't tell my wife this, but just now you made me feel so powerful and attractive, that I almost wanted to have my way with you."

Sasha laughed and replied, "You are not ready for that, Mr. President. Besides, you know we conservative Republican women don't break up homes; we make them."

He left the bathroom and began to walk toward the conference room, passing by numerous members of his inner circle. As he walked past each person, he was energized by his flashback and the phrases he had running through his mind. Like all confident and powerful men, he was invigorated by the admiration others had for him and he gave them each a nod with his chest out. It was as if he was peacocking to everyone around him for what he was about to do; his demeanor had to be nothing short of amazing. He was about to enter a room filled with lions, and he knew if he projected anything short of confidence, they would only test him. Perception was going to be his first line of defense. As he approached the door of the conference room, he was met by four men who scanned his retinas and fingerprints. He looked ahead and raised his arms in preparation for a full-body weapons scan.

"It's been a long time since I've been checked like this. There must be some very important people in that room," he said jokingly in order to ease the tension.

The man conducting the search smirked and replied, "And you must be the most important one, since you are the last one in and the meeting hasn't started without you."

Once the scans were completed, Johnson opened the door in grand fashion, with his hands on both of the handles and pushing the double doors as far as they could go with his arms fully extended. The thick and heavy mahogany doors swung open so wide an elephant could fit through them. The people already seated in the room turned their heads in unison and stared at him in awe as if he entered the room with fireworks shooting off in the air.

"Gentlemen and ladies, we are here because we have a situation, a situation never seen before in the history of humankind. A situation that will vilify some of you and make heroes out of the rest of you. And today, we find out which ones you are going to be. The circumstances are bleak but within our control. We are empowered to save this planet, and none of us in this room can allow their morality to limit our privilege to stay alive and sustain humanity on this planet. If any of you allow your personal feelings to impact our dilemma and that privilege, we will experience catastrophic events the world has never seen before."

Johnson realized that powerful people can get scared as well and that to hit them hard and fast was the best thing to do in order to keep them off their guard and be the leader they needed in this situation. "To speak bluntly, we are here because we have a real fucking problem! And, fellow leaders, please excuse my language because I am not just saying that to be provocative.

The world is reproducing too much and dying off too slowly, so we are here to find solutions to address the number one issue our generation will ever face. Because if we don't, it will be truly the end of the world. As you all have been briefed before you arrived here…"

Before the president could finish his sentence, he was interrupted by Roderik Von Merchant, the chancellor of Germany.

"Briefed? What do you mean briefed? I am not sure about the others, but I was only told this would be a short meeting to discuss population control after the funeral for Perez and that is it. If you consider that to be a briefing, then I need to leave because this meeting is going to be a waste of my time. Furthermore, you have us waiting over ten minutes, and then you come into this room using your vulgar American language as if we are in some pub. This is outrageous!"

Merchant was trying his best to stay seated and not slam on the table as he was known to do in the German Parliament. Johnson knew immediately that Merchant was going to be a problem and quickly turned his tone down and his attention toward the angry German.

"Chancellor, you are right, and I apologize to you and anyone else in this room I may have offended. It was merely my intention to emphasize how we have arrived at our current predicament."

Merchant and Johnson locked eyes, with Johnson projecting sincere humility toward Merchant. Johnson couldn't care less about Merchant, and there wasn't a sincere bone in his body toward any of the other people in the room, but he knew that all of these leaders were vital to this meeting. Losing any of them over a petty misunderstanding would prove to be disastrous to the long-term goals he set for this meeting.

Johnson regained the attention of the room once Merchant sat down, and he continued speaking. "As I was saying, the United States has been aware of this issue for over thirty years, and we began a covert campaign in Africa to try to solve it. Now, what I am about to tell you will alarm many of you in this room, and once you hear what I am about to say, your life as you know it will never be the same. As leaders of your nations, you are only here because you possess nuclear weapons, but in 1982, Ronald Reagan implemented a weapon system far more advanced than any nuclear weapon in the history of the world. The weapon system was called Operation Storm Cloud. The world was told that Reagan peacefully negotiated with Russia regarding the Berlin Wall, but that is completely false. Gorbachev allowed the Berlin Wall to come down because he had no choice after he was told about Operation Storm Cloud. Gorbachev was forced to allow the wall to come down because he learned that the United States actually blew up Chernobyl and used Operation Storm Cloud to contain the nuclear fallout. Once we showed the USSR our capability, the Cold War officially ended, and we have been implementing democracy throughout the world ever since."

"What is this Operation Storm Cloud?" asked Merchant.

President Johnson walked over to Russian President Vadim Alexandrov and placed his hands on the other man's shoulders in sympathy. Johnson then addressed the others. "The weapon's implementation was in 1981, but the groundwork began in the 1960s. The United States achieved full control of weather in 1982, but in order for us to successfully use the weapon, we had to place parts of the mechanism in specific points throughout

11

the world. Our wars with Korea, Iraq, and Vietnam plus our conflicts with Bosnia, Columbia, and Liberia and our strategic alliances with Japan and Israel have enabled us to install these mechanisms. Over the last thirty years, we have been concentrating 'the effect' primarily in one continent: Africa. We have been systematically controlling that population of sava..." Johnson paused as he thought better of fully saying the slur, especially with Merchant so ready to take control of the room and the fear of offending others.

"...Africans for the last thirty years, but not solely with Operation Storm Cloud. The droughts were an example, but the implementation of the AIDS virus and other biological creations were all us. As you all can imagine, hiding it took a substantial amount of effort. We promoted government instability by limiting imports and strategically financing coups and civil unrest, even famine. We have done this for the past thirty years, but they just keep reproducing. By our estimates, had we not instituted the famine in Ethiopia in 1986, the killings in Darfur and the Congo, and the uprising in Egypt, we would have had this problem twenty years ago."

Merchant interrupted, "You still have not told us what the problem is!"

He was growing uneasy with Merchant's constant outbursts, but Johnson finished his thought. "Because of its population size, we had no choice but to include China into the equation, but we had to wait until China was capable of being an ally with this effort, so we strategically poured economic stimulus into that country, to build a stable government with a prosperous economy. But, as their economy has gotten bigger, so has their population, so we assisted them with the implementation of the one child per couple rule. As China became bigger and grew more powerful, so did their aspirations."

Johnson paused and looked directly into Prime Minister Jiang Yo's eyes as he placed both of his hands on the table and leaned forward. Both men stared each other down like boxers while Johnson continued. "Now, what I am about to say should serve as a warning to any of you in this room who will try to copy this technology. Despite all of our efforts to maintain a peaceful existence with China—no, a peaceful existence with the world—in 2013, we discovered that China had tried to implement its own technology to counteract Operation Storm

Cloud. Once we found this out, within one summer, we introduced Thailand to floods, the Philippines to Typhoon Haiyan, and Australia to extreme summer temperatures. Make no mistake; the United States will be the only nation to possess this weapon, and any nation that tries to copy our technology will be dealt with accordingly."

"Why didn't the U.S. just deal with China directly? Why attack other nations that have nothing to do with China just so you can prove a point to them?" asked Prime Minister Aaron Yuzary of Israel.

"At the time, China had too many financial ties to the United States. If we created a disaster strong enough to match our intent that may have forced China to panic and sell those financial ties causing a fiscal panic similar to the one we experienced just 6 years before with the Great Recession. My government's mission was to never let our economy prevent us from acting to save the world, so to prevent that from ever occurring again, we no longer have uncontrolled debt to any nation. Now that I have everyone's full attention, let me state this: there is no way to steal or develop this weather technology. If you try, we will show you *directly* what we showed China *indirectly.* Each of you is here for one reason and one reason only: the United States needs you to share in the responsibility of fixing this population issue, and fast.

You have been asked to come here because after years of controversy and billions of dollars spent on scientific research, the United States government has discovered the cause of the global climate changes. With people living longer and humanity's insatiable desire for material possessions, the planet is literally unable to sustain its own weight. The weight of the world has resulted in the Earth moving off of its orbital path and away from the sun. We are now charged with finding a sustainable solution to this problem. You are here to follow orders and to get rid of everything not nailed to the floor. And when I say 'everything,' I mean people, buildings, cars; ANYTHING because today we must start the process of deciding who should live and who should die and to do that we will begin with a world war.

Once that war has been completed, each of you will select a group to attack in your homeland. This group can be one of your choosing: gay, straight, black, white, purple, or brown. I don't care. But once the war has concluded, your population must be reduced by fifteen percent within five years. After five years, we all will lead a unified effort to erase the Arab world in the Middle East and Africa. All remaining Muslims not in Africa will be migrated to Africa, and our nations will colonize the Middle East for oil. Turkey will be spared. By reducing our population, we will reduce the weight of the world. We cannot fail! All South American nations and Australia will be safe havens, meaning those nations will be excluded from the first round of war, but they will be required to reduce their population the same as everyone else once the war has concluded. Friends, to be clear, the United States is already in the process of implementing its domestic strategy, and we have selected the individual who will be the face of our plan. I personally want to assure the rest of you that this matter is of grave importance. To emphasize how important this issue is, once the war has concluded, we will begin testing our remaining population for sickness and disease. Any citizen of the United States who is ill in any way, whether mental or physical, will be eliminated. Our prescription drug database allows us to accurately track who is using anything from heart medication to pills for depression. Those individuals utilizing any medications will be singled out accordingly."

"But I take pills for depression from time to time," interrupted Russian President Alexandrov.

Johnson looked at Alexandrov. "Well, be happy you are on this side of the door."

He then took his focus off of Alexandrov and continued to address the entire room. "The family members of these 'sacrificed' individuals will be compensated by our government via the Ward Health Elimination Act. Since President Obama implemented universal healthcare in 2013, we have lost a substantial amount of money because we are treating everyone. The money we save from not treating those individuals will be allocated to the affected families. We will provide you all with details once that time comes. Gentlemen and women, I know this sounds harsh, but we are leaders! Leaders make tough decisions. These decisions will impact and test your faith and values, but this world must go on, and your responsibility will be to ensure that and nothing else. This war will have to be fought differently; we cannot pollute the earth any more than we already have. Energy resources that release toxins into the air such as oil, coal, and nuclear power will be destroyed, and we will provide your countries with the technology to rebuild by using only water. In 2012, President Obama allowed more offshore drilling than at any other time in history. Those rigs were never pumping oil. They were a filtration system that funneled the seawater to a base in Kentucky. The water at the base is used to power the entire eastern seaboard of the country. This technology separates the salt from the water; it is then crystallized to be used for building materials. We have never released this technology because humans are incapable of moderation. If the world had known about this technology, we would have drained the sea by now."

"We refill the used water by causing massive hurricanes out at sea. The floods in Thailand were caused when our human-made storm mixed with a naturally generated storm. We realized that the weather system was altered because the earth's orbit is changing."

Johnson paused and asked, "Does anyone have any questions?"

He looked at the face of Prime Minister David Wiltshire of Britain, which was nothing short of horrified. Once he realized how overwhelming all this information was for them, he continued, not because he wanted to, but because he didn't want any interruptions. Johnson always felt that interruptions created questions, and the fact that no one in the room had interrupted him meant he would be able to tell them anything and they would do it. When he worked at Morgan Stanley after he graduated from college, he was barely able to get through a presentation due to questions. He would receive a thousand questions not because his information was wrong but because all the people in the room wanted his job. They wanted to be in the front of the room, the center of attention. This was not the case in the briefing room. No one wanted to switch positions with him, at any costs.

"Now before we get down to the logistics, please note that America is willing to lose the war in order to make this partnership work. If your people see how mighty your governments are by defeating America, they will be more willing to honor your government. We will instruct our media to spin any loss into a 'compromised withdrawal' because the people of my nation are easily influenced through strategic propaganda and unwavering patriotism. With most of the major media outlets being owned by five mega corporations, we will be able to sell any message to the American people that we choose. In return, we will provide those companies with tax breaks. What you will not be able to do is gloat about it! If we encounter large-scale disrespect, our interests throughout the world will be compromised, and that will be cause for us to destroy you, not because we want to but because we still need to manage our image. Gentlemen and women, America will lose, but we will lead. To further demonstrate how much our image means to us, if you gloat in any way or turn against us, we will focus Operation Storm Cloud on your crops, hindering your ability to feed your people by causing either extreme drought or flooding. Nothing speeds up the destruction of a nation like starvation. Under dire circumstances, rich men will sell their daughters if it puts food on their tables."

Before Johnson could get another word out of his mouth, the communist leader of China, Jiang Yo, interrupted, "President Johnson, we are clear on what you are saying. But don't insult us with your continuous undertones of how much of a choice we have with this Operation Storm Cloud. We really don't have a choice! America has no equal for now, and no one in this room can stop you, so stop pretending to negotiate with us because we are in fact hostages. The only reason I have not taken a swing at you is because I am too old, and I sense the sincerity in your voice that this issue is dire."

Little did the other leaders in the room know that Yo already knew who he wanted gone. In a surprise move to everyone in the room, he continued, stating, "North Korea must go!"

Everyone in the room stared at him with shock.

"Please forgive me, Your Excellency, but isn't North Korea one of your closest allies?" asked Prime Minister Aaron Yuzary from Israel.

"They are, but they refuse to improve. Forty years ago, I went to them with the idea of cooperation for the betterment of our nations." Yo took a short pause before he finished his sentence, as if he was reflecting on the very day he approached North Korea. "*Both* of our nations. I instructed them to follow our path through education and modified isolationism, and they rejected my offer. Instead, they chose to be reliant and dependent. We have tried to finance several energy methods with them, and they were unsuccessful because of their leadership. Once we realized Dictator Bong-hwa Om would never fully embrace this idea, we began to secretly finance revolutionists, so they would need us to come to their rescue. Once they continued asking for help, we were able dictate terms. The same way you are doing to us." Yo looked at Johnson straight in the eyes.

"As you can see by the current state of North Korea, we were not able to implement all the terms we had liked. Because both of our countries lack resources, we have been developing our own technology to hunt for oil reserves without digging by using infrared beams produced by satellites we launched decades ago. Back in 2013, when tensions between the United States and my country were rising over the air rights in the East China Sea, we did not take a stand over airplanes flying over the region; we took a stand against the United States because the base for our technology was stationed underground there. But after hearing about your new weaponry, I am ashamed. Here we were trying to invent technology to find old forms of resources to power my nation while you Americans are using seawater for renewable energy. But that is something I will have to deal with on my own."

Johnson was growing impatient with Yo talking and interrupted. "Is there a point you are trying to make with this, Your Excellency?"

"Yes, there is a point. Our technology has discovered that North Korea has oil reserves that exceed those of any other country in the world. It's such a huge supply that I would like to have it. If America is willing to show its faith in this endeavor, I ask that North Korea side with you in the war. Then when America loses, the surrender package includes releasing North Korea under our full control with the United States backing China with the reconstruction."

"That's not a problem, but why not just do that now? You are already their ally; how would you suggest we spin this?" replied Johnson.

Yo firmly stated, "I will provide you with directions for that, but we will take over the North Korean government and implement a Western influence of technology and infrastructure there once the transfer is complete."

"Wow! Your Excellency, it didn't take too much to get you on board. But as I told you, we have technology to end oil dependence. Why do you need the oil?" asked Johnson.

"Mr. President, the United States has its secrets; we have ours. So let's just leave it at that," replied Yo.

"That is fine as long as we are in agreement that oil dependence will be done within twenty years of the end of the war," said Johnson firmly.

Yo nodded in agreement. Yo thought the president was bluffing the whole time regarding the true power of Operation Storm Cloud, but he also knew that Johnson was a reactive individual who would do anything to maintain control of the room including proving a point to get the others in line. Yo did not want to take the chance that Johnson would do something that would negatively affect China, so he thought remaining silent despite his intuition would be the best course of action. Negotiating with Johnson first in front of the others in the room would ensure Yo's legacy in the minds of the Chinese people. Winning a war against the United States and ensuring oil reserves for his country once the war started was critical. He felt that despite the available technology pertaining to seawater, the Americans' infrastructure was decades away from utilizing it in their everyday activities. He wanted to hedge America's potential of becoming dependent on buying oil from the Chinese until the transition was complete.

"OK, here we are. Now it's time to pick sides the same way we did back in the schoolyard. This will be random, with each side having a member in its alliance with a totally different sociopolitical affiliation. As stated, the United States will have North Korea, and China will have Canada," said Johnson.

"Why Canada?" asked Canadian Prime Minister Abigail Bennett, who was the first female prime minister since A. Kim Campbell.

"I need this close to home, Bennett, to sell it to my people." Johnson was surprised that Bennett was the only person to step up and ask a question. He continued to survey the room and figured he'd wait for them to absorb what they had been hearing. Yo was the first to respond with demands, and Johnson respected him for speaking up, but he was not going to easily agree with anyone else going forward. Johnson's eyebrow was raised toward Yo now, and he began to wonder what Yo had up his sleeve as he mentally made a note to maintain an eye on him during this process. Something just seemed fishy, but with the Chinese on board, the rest of the nations were going to line up easily. The dilemma now was that everyone knew that the outcome of the war was fixed; how was he going sell to the other leaders the benefit of being on the losing side of the war? In war, losing means the winner gets to write the history about you. It also means your nation sustains more damage, and the loss of life is usually more substantial. The lives of the leaders and their family names will be destroyed forever. Selling a war usually means someone has to be painted as the bad guy, and that person usually goes the way of the dodo bird and Saddam Hussein. Yo offering up North Korea was perfect for Johnson. Not in a million years would he have thought of what Yo so willingly suggested.

Johnson had never been a thorough leader, but he was a great evaluator of talent and personalities, which had enabled him to have a strong cast around throughout his entire life. With this scenario, he couldn't have written a better ticket for himself and his legacy. America coming to the aid of an arch enemy and then losing because of it would allow Johnson, who was always an extreme isolationist at heart, to do what he had longed to do since he became a politician: close the doors of America. Johnson always felt that wars couldn't be fought now the way they were fought during World War II. With the financial markets, jobs, the Internet, and the accessibility of international travel, we were all connected. How do you tell the CEO of Citibank to close bank branches in a particular country they do business in when that will cost John and Jane Smith their jobs in America? Johnson knew he could not because it would be impossible to segregate expenses and income made in one country and be headquartered in another.

Johnson resented the fact that America was spending astronomical amounts of taxpayer dollars on defense every year and could not utilize all of the weapons by going to war because of the potential for an administrative nightmare as well as the economic consequences. Blowing up a building in 1942 didn't have the same results as blowing up that same building in the present day. With servers, electronic information, equipment, and reduced natural resources, rebuilding was 100 percent more complicated. The idea was so stimulating to Johnson that he began to imagine how he would rationalize the destruction by telling Americans that the new structure would be environmentally friendlier than the old structure. Johnson's fantasizing did not stop at his rationalizations. He began envisioning himself advocating for isolation via speeches to the nation. He would tell the American people that because of the war, we couldn't afford to police outside of our boarders, and we must pay our debt and rebuild by expanding domestic manufacturing and closing our borders to protect us from Canada and Mexico, which he gladly gave up to China to sell this war. The meeting was only an hour old, and the kings of the chessboard were starting to show themselves while the pawns were still wondering what side they would be on.

Yo knew Johnson had something up his sleeve just as he did, but the next steps here were critical to secure the uneasy truce.

Just before Yo opened his mouth again, President Alexandrov, upset about the whole ordeal screamed out, "How dare you, Johnson? You sit back, and you tell us what to do, and we just sit here and accept it. As you arrogant Americans say, who the fuck do you think you are? Don't count us in. I am leaving this meeting!"

"Alexandrov, please rethink this," Johnson replied calmly.

"No! I am leaving!" screamed Alexandrov.

Johnson picked up the phone and pressed the speaker button so the entire room could hear the conversation. "This is President Johnson. GW forty-six, lowercase A D."

The voice over the phone replied, "You are cleared to go."

"One second," said the president. Johnson turned to his computer and Googled the longitude and latitude of President Alexandrov's house in Russia. "The coordinates are 71.05480 by 52.005048. Let's have lightning strikes thirty seconds apart and at half power. I don't want the structure totally destroyed. Who knows what's in there?" Johnson turned to the satellite system on the large screen in the center of the room. He then turned to Alexandrov and stared at him with no emotion as he watched Alexandrov witness the destruction of the east wing of his presidential home.

Alexandrov looked stunned as Johnson then turned to a Russian news channel so that Alexandrov could get confirmation of the weapon's power.

"Alexandrov, why are you in such a hurry if you don't have a home to go to?" said Johnson. "Yo has a home to go to. I have a home to go to. Abigail has a home to go to, but you don't.

That's odd because we all have so much in common. We all have power. We all have money. We all have personal assistants. And yet you don't have a home. All these others still have a home because they understand what may be potentially at stake. Instead of acting hastily and not thinking your actions through, know that your lack of participation will have consequences. Consequences that weren't even necessary if you just cooperated. And for that, you are on my team, and we will lose this war."

As Johnson was talking, Yo was reflecting on how his instincts were right. Johnson was going to make an example of someone regardless, not because he wanted to, but because he had to so he could impose his will on the others and validate everything he had been saying. As Yo began to come out of his reflection, he realized that Johnson was still talking.

"Gentlemen and ladies, I assure you this problem is real. But as real as it is, it's correctable. Make no mistake, the earth is spinning out of orbit because we have to get rid of massive amounts of weight. We could have attempted this on our own without you, but we realize we cannot do this alone. This is a world effort, and the people in this room are the only ones who have the power to do something about it not just for today but for the future, and the actions of one person cannot jeopardize the lives of billions of people."

As Johnson glanced over, he wanted to apologize to Alexandrov, but he just couldn't do it. He needed to look strong in front of the other leaders, and empathy at that moment would create confusion. Alexandrov, anxious to get on the phone, was also scared to contact his homeland, wondering if his wife and kids were in that house.

Johnson relieved Alexandrov's anxiety by saying, "Alexandrov, please go and get in contact with your country, and don't worry about your family. One of your secret service agents is with us, and he was instructed to vacate your family immediately before we hit the building. And so you don't think that we just singled you out, know we have ensured that all of your families are being protected by one of our own, and if we weren't able to get someone to infiltrate your security details, we would have planned a diversion to have your families evacuated. Now we must move on."

The mood of the room immediately became intense as everyone felt powerless to voice any resistance to Johnson. For each leader the only thing left to do was what Johnson instructed, and that was to begin to address selecting the sides for war. Each leader began to carefully plot out his or her next move, knowing that Mexico and Canada were on one side and the United States, North Korea, and Russia were on the other.

"I have a question, King Johnson—I mean, President Johnson," said Chancellor Merchant.

Johnson smiled at the chancellor's sarcasm as he replied, "Please, Chancellor Merchant, do ask."

Merchant acknowledged Johnson and said, "This war...I understand why it's required, but at what point will it end? How much death, or in this case weight, will be enough? If the plan is to be implemented properly, then your country with its vast amount of material or weight—not people but your cars, your homes, your boats, your skyscrapers—would be at risk as much as anyone else's."

"We did think of that, which is why Canada and Mexico have to be against us in this war. Sending troops to Asia and leaving our lands open to attack will solve that issue. Buildings will be leveled, cities will be attacked from the north and south, and property will be destroyed. Once the war has concluded, social and political change will be more acceptable from a weight standpoint. The population of China and India must be dramatically reduced. The caste systems in place would be a natural rule of execution, leaving just enough people to rebuild." The president paused due to a woman entering the room with booklets in her hands.

"What Christina is going to hand to you are booklets that contain the calculations of what your country's weight needs to be. These calculations are extreme because it will take eight months for the earth to get back into its original orbit once the weight reduction is achieved. Then we must maintain the weight for another six months so that the Sun's gravitational pull sustains the orbit. Any landmarks that are kept have to be included in your country's weight budgets based on your current amounts. For example, if France wants to keep the Eiffel Tower, that amount of weight must be accounted for by reduction of persons, places, or things of the same weight. Countries in violation of this will have economic sanctions imposed against them, and I am not talking that UN nonsense; I am talking about bush fires and hurricanes. For countries that do not comply, by the time we are done your citizens won't even be able to get an insurance policy. Now, I know I sound very harsh, but at the end of the day it's about us, about humanity. You are not in this room because we needed to have a party. You are in here to save the Earth. Our very existence is at stake! Now speaking of the Eiffel tower…President Garçon, I pick you. Germany, you are with China."

President Anton Garçon was a tall, good-looking man with dark hair and brown eyes, but he was clearly in over his head. Elected because he was a former soccer player with tremendous intellect, his advocacy and enforcement of gay rights and equal partnerships worldwide and via UN sanctions had the whole world wondering if he was gay. And being elected as the only single man in French history did not help dispute those thoughts. Garçon looked up at the others and felt it was his time to assert himself into the conversation, but before he could get a word out, Chancellor Merchant agreed with President Johnson's suggestion.

"I don't want that nancy anywhere near me, so it would be my pleasure to send troops to destroy those French faggots!"

Merchant was notorious for his conservative views regarding race, sexuality, and every other social issue. Despite winning the chancellorship under the Christian Social Union of Bavaria party, there had been rumors that he was a founding member of the Pro Germany Citizens' Movement also known as the PGC during his teenage years. Once the party had enough support to enter the political realm, the rumors making Merchant one of the founding members of the party increased, but no one was willing to provide confirmation of that. The truth has always been that after his dad was killed by getting hit by a car while chasing an immigrant 12 year old girl who pickpocketed him, he founded the group in the basement of his home.

Since the girl was 12 and German law considered her a minor, she was never prosecuted because of her age and with the girl not being able to speak German she was never punished. Liberals in the country actually felt sorry for the girl and adopted her, which allowed her to obtain great sympathy for her situation and she was later able to attend the best universities in the country. This enraged Merchant and helped him develop the core values of the party which advocated for complete law and order and lowering the age of criminal responsibility from 14 to 12 years of age. Merchant also wanted the deportation of illegal immigrants as well as the segregation of students unable to speak German. Since his father was a German banker, Merchant honored his life by being critical of multi-national banks, corporations and other financial institutions.

With Germany experiencing an economic depression because they took on too much of the European Union's debt during the Economic Recession of 2013, his rise to power was easy as he painted his opponent as weak and not willing to put the German people first. German polls showed the people had no problem with shouldering the load, but they wanted the power to match the risk. Wilhelm Brandt, the grandson of Angela Merkel in the Christian Democratic Union party, did not want the European Union to get nervous as they did during World War II, so he did not ask for extras in order to seem accommodative and trustworthy. Merchant exploited that mistake, which led to his election.

Garçon replied in French, "Pardon?"

Merchant responded, "Speak English, so we all can understand. And I called you a faggot!"

Garçon stood up and pointed his finger in Merchant's face. Merchant slapped Garçon's hand from his face and stood up as well. Merchant was about three inches shorter than Garçon, but his rage and confidence equalized Garçon's height advantage.

"The whole world knows you are gay. For you to sit at this table, which is filled with great men and women, and pretend to be their equal is an insult to me. To make you surrender would be my pleasure," screamed Merchant.

"You idiot. The fight is fixed. Germany making France surrender under normal circumstances wouldn't even be possible today. My people ache for the chance to avenge World War II. And why do you think I am gay? Just because I think all people regardless of sexual preference should have the right to live their lives without politicians imposing their view, religion, or propaganda on them? Better yet, how about you ask your ugly wife whether I am gay or not? The way she looks at me, I can tell she wants to find out!" shouted Garçon.

Merchant's face was beet red. He was doing everything he could to prevent himself from going after Garçon until his rage overtook him and he couldn't take it. Merchant leaped over the table and attacked Garçon. Merchant's move was so surprising and sudden that no one could stop it, and Garçon and Merchant were engaged, each trying to overpower the other to gain an advantage while they wrestled on the floor. Merchant was so enraged and filled with adrenaline that he nearly overwhelmed Garçon to punch him in the face, but Garçon used his momentum to push him over and pinned him down.

"Look at you, so filled with emotion you are barely thinking straight. Your rationale has left you, and it's resulted in you being in this very position, which is why Germany would never beat France again. Its leader is…is…Captain something. What's that story with the whale?" asked Garçon as he looked up at the others in the room for affirmation.

The guards walked in the room and looked at Johnson, who gave them a signal not to break up the fight because he was secretly enjoying watching it. Although Johnson was delighted about the fight, he acted apprehensively and answered the question. "Captain Ahab."

"Oh yes, Captain Ahab," Garçon repeated sarcastically as he continued to stay on top of Merchant, with Merchant getting more and more frustrated because he was pinned down.

Garçon continued, "Are you so antigay because deep down you secretly are gay and are longing for the touch of a man, wanting to feel a man's lips?" Merchant looked visibly sickened as he closed his eyes tight in disgust and shifted his head to the left with the right side of his face touching the floor. Garçon, knowing he was getting to Merchant, continued to aggravate him. "Sorry, mi amore. I can't be that man because I am not gay, but I will help you."

Garçon put his right leg over Merchant's left arm and used his left hand to straighten Merchant's face so that the two of them were eye to eye. He then bent down and kissed Merchant on the mouth.

"You see, you homophobe. That wasn't so bad," said Garçon in a nonchalant manner. Then he bent over to Merchant's ear and whispered so that only the two of them could hear, "I know that doesn't compare to Fehrenbach."

Merchant's face went from anger to total shock as he realized that Garçon knew about his secret. Then Garçon let Merchant up and straightened out his clothes.

"Sorry, everyone, that you had to witness this misunderstanding, but I think we are, as they say in the States, all good now."

Once Garçon got off of Merchant, Johnson immediately realized he could use the encounter as a way to influence how the war would start with German and France. Barely able to contain his excitement, he said, "Everyone, I think we have our reason for the war in Europe to begin. Merchant will begin killing and exiling gays in Germany. France will offer all of the exiled Germans shelter and immediately grant them French citizenship. Germany will consider this as an act of war because the French are intervening in their affairs. Germany will also accuse France of stealing Germany's best citizens because not all the exiles are gay; they also include people who do not want to be separated from their families. Germany will use that as the rationalization to attack several 'acceptance stations' on French soil. Germany will begin winning the war at the start, and America will side with France in the name of democracy, which will result in China coming to Germany's rescue and forcing the allegiance between the two. America coming to the defense of France will force the other European nations to choose a side, and we will be well on our way to solving our little weight issue."

"But, Johnson, if you are wrong about this, and France is unable to rebuild for the future, I will personally choke you to death," said Garçon.

All the leaders in the room were in total awe of Garçon. Until that day, all of them thought he was soft and secretly disassociated their nations from France. Now, in one instance, that all changed. They began to admire him like the nerdy kid who stood up to and beat the bully in the lunchroom.

Feeling the same way as all the others in the room, Johnson replied, "Wow, Garçon. I didn't think you had that in you! You have truly surprised me, old boy! And to answer your *threat*, with one hundred percent certainty you will be able to rebuild. I don't even like half of you in this room, so I would not have brought you here if it wasn't necessary and if life couldn't go back to normal once this is complete."

Johnson had a way of saying whatever he thought, and most of the other leaders both loved and hated him for it, but they all knew that what you see is what you get with him. Johnson then turned to Wiltshire and said, "You don't think I see the wheels turning, son? Are you going to sit there in amazement, or are you going to get in the game?"

Johnson always knew that Wiltshire admired him, and he used that to his advantage at every opportunity he could. Johnson's running joke when the prime minister came to visit America was, "You know why relations between England and America are so great? Because Wiltshire does whatever I say and, in turn, I reward him by treating him like he has a chance to have a friendship with me."

Wiltshire always longed for Johnson's approval, and this meeting was no different.

"We have problems with minorities in England. Some are great, and others depend on social entitlement programs and have no desire to improve themselves. Any suggestions on how we can satisfy the problem by adding it to our agenda?" asked Wiltshire.

Johnson looked at him with disgust. Most of the time he threw jabs at Wiltshire so that Wiltshire could stand up against him as if he was a mother lion training her cub to hunt. But with Wiltshire basically asking Johnson to help him kill these people without taking responsibility, he had reached his limit.

"What are we, mercenaries? I am not the godfather granting wishes on my daughter's wedding day, so don't come at me that way. No one here is at fault for what has happened with the earth, but we are accountable for fixing it. Wiltshire, I am saying this to you so that you know: there are no bad guys in this room. This war is for the greater good of the planet, and our survival depends on it. If you want some minorities gone but not all of them, then say so. There are no easy decisions with this, but we must be decisive and prepare our consciences that this is for the greater good. Don't look to the next person in the room to do your dirty work so that you can sleep at night because there will be a lot of sleep lost in the coming years!"

Wiltshire looked perplexed and just as he was about to speak, the Japanese prime minister, Yoshihiko Kan, began to speak. "I am all for ethnic cleansing, but let's face it, my nation has smarter people than most of the other nations in this room. I can see where Wiltshire is going, but he is…how do you say? He is too scared to say it, so I will. We need a standardized test for all nations. Only the smartest people will be able to live once the war is over."

Wiltshire added, "Prime Minister Kan, if the Japanese are so smart why are they always in a financial crisis?"

Kan looked up at Wiltshire as if he was about to explain and Wiltshire continued speaking as if nothing Kan could say would be a good enough answer. "Despite Kan's misconception of his people, I agree with him and we don't want the smart people killed in the war. We must use this war as the first wave of removal. Standardized testing would be another wave of removal. We can make the testing mandatory, but the results must be given on that day, so we can execute the lower levels that day since they will be in test-taking facilities. Test takers will be given bracelets, so we can identify those who take the test. The ones who skip the test will be killed on sight, once we establish a universal day when we expect everyone on Earth to take the test."

"Johnson, do your projections evaluate even distribution of weight?" asked Kan.

"What do you mean?" replied Johnson.

"Say all the people in America are below standard and all the people in Japan are above standard, and we eliminate all the people in America and keep all the people in Japan. Will that force the earth out of orbit, since one portion of the earth is heavier than the other, sort of like a Libra scale?" asked Kan.

"Based on past acts of war, we have concluded that won't be an issue. Each country will have to share human resources to make this work, because at the end of the day, we will need to keep the lights on so society can function. So things such as shared immigration will have to be an option," said Johnson.

Wiltshire offered a suggestion that seemed to be on everyone's mind. "What about slavery? Can we implement slavery again? We can get a labor force from Africa and Mexico. We can offer citizenship based on labor and provide small examples of success by making certain individuals of the slave class rich, to give the labor force hope and ambition so they can work harder."

Wiltshire's suggestion resulted in Mexican President Felipe Zedillo giving him a menacing stare, but Zedillo knew he was in no position to protest, since the cartels had completely overrun the Mexican government and 30 percent of the nation. Realizing this, Zedillo tried to use this opportunity to negotiate for the future by asking a question. "I do have one question. What are we going to do with the bodies? Dead bodies still weigh the same for a certain amount of time until they are fully decomposed. Even though they are dead, the earth will still weigh the same. Also, I don't appreciate your suggestion for using my nation as slaves. We are capable of so much more!" he said as he looked at Witlshire.

Before Withshire could respond, Johnson began to speak, "First, let's be clear Felipe, you are here because of your country's location and this war and nothing more. Mexico is as useful as a pregnant prostitute. If we did have a slave population, your country would have some use because we could use the drugs to control the slave labor by keeping them dependent. Once we destroy everything in your country, we could use the Mexicans to rebuild it and we will implement a stronger government headed by you and free of the cartels. Second, there is some weird thing these geeks at MIT told me about the law of conservation of mass. The stuff is too high level for me to fully comprehend, but it basically states that matter can be changed from one form into another, mixtures can be separated or made, and pure substances can be decomposed, but the total amount of mass remains constant. So, even if we cremated the bodies or let the bodies decompose, the weight on the world would still be the same, so we will have to send the bodies into space. In fact, everything needs to go into space including building materials. We will even have to dig up graveyards and remove those bodies as well, but once we get to that, it will be fine. The war will be over, and this phase will have begun. Our main focus will be to maintain the banks and make sure the remaining people still believe in currency. It's a tough reality with tough choices. This is a win-win for you and your people. You will finally be able to govern your nation without the threat of your head being cut off by some twelve-year-old trained to be a hit man by the cartel leaders. But, to answer your question, dead bodies will have to go into space," said Johnson in an annoyed manner.

"I understand, but wouldn't sending bodies into space alert the world to what is going on? Families like to mourn their dead loved ones, you know," responded Zedillo.

Johnson paused to gather his thoughts and take a deep breath because he honestly despised everything about Mexico, and it was well known because of his campaign promises of defending the borders. After the DREAM Act was enacted during the Chelsea Clinton administration, Johnson was able to win as the first Republican in over three decades because he secretly sent out pamphlets to the residents of border states with the title "Strong Leadership Against the Invaders of the South."

Once he finished gathering his thoughts and was about to continue, the prime minister of Canada, Abigail Bennett, said, "The belief in the currency is the key, but the banking system is already too strong. We have to find a way to limit its power in this process as well. But once we start killing off people with wars, we have to compensate the banks for the loss of loan payments and financial instruments."

"Since all of our countries will be saving money based on the reduction of healthcare and entitlement programs, we can compensate the banks by paying them the balance of the loan at the time of death, not for the life of the loans. The world bailed them out in 2008 and 2013, and I will be damned if we don't bring that up once we involve them, but I know those greedy liars will ask for the interest as well. We will also need them to freeze the assets of the individuals who have not taken the test and hold those funds for their family members, should those people not have wills," replied Johnson.

"Speaking of money, are we setting a price to be able to buy your way out of going to war or failing the test?" asked Alexandrov.

"I am glad you are on board with us," replied Johnson sarcastically.

But before Alexandrov could respond, Merchant screamed out, "I am opposed to that wholeheartedly! The rich have been using their money to get passes since the beginning of time, and we need to put an end to that!"

"Relax there, chief," said Johnson. "Rich folks are OK when you need them to fund your campaign, but not to save their own lives? That's not going to stop even with this major instance.

We will set the price at two million dollars and, to keep the price fair, we will use the currency valued at the highest amount six months from today."

"I don't understand. What do you mean?" asked Merchant.

"Meaning, I don't want to set it at any nation's currency now because two million US dollars could be worth more or less than two million euros once this process begins, resulting people in Europe or America being able to purchase their freedom at a bargain price. So, whatever nation in the world has the highest currency value in six months, two million dollars of that currency will be able to buy your life. Any nation caught trying to influence their currency value in any way will be subject to weight limit reductions and loss of a national treasure during the war. So if Canada is caught manipulating the currency, say good-bye to the CN Tower and hello to reductions of millions of pounds. The members of the losing nations will get a discount for their citizens. The funds from all nations—meaning winners and nonparticipating nations whose citizens pay the full price—will be used to finance rebuilding efforts and compensate the banks for lost revenue," explained Johnson.

Garçon was amazed at how powerful men have the capabilities to come up with plans for destruction and rebuilding in such a short period of time. The swiftness was mesmerizing and scary for him, but a feeling of relief came over him. In France, the whole room would have been looking to him for answers, testing him, ready to second-guess him at every turn. In this room, he felt they were all in this together regardless of how much power America actually had. No one person would shoulder the load alone. On this occasion, they would be the pallbearers with the casket on each of their shoulders instead of solely on one person's back. Garçon was conflicted with the idea of any citizen being able to buy his or her life, but as a master of world history, he realized that this mind-set had sustained the world throughout its existence. What would be the point of saying anything against allowing the rich to buy their freedom if he realized that once the "new earth" was established, it would be less dangerous? Plus, he didn't want to admit that he was agreeing with Merchant on anything. The bad blood between the two of them ran deep, and he would be against anything Merchant believed in no matter the consequences. People hate the rich, but the great thing about the rich is they want to keep order; they want to keep things the same, so they can continue to live their lives in the lap of luxury. Any disruption to that ideology makes them nervous. Garçon embraced the notion that once the war ended, the world was going to be less dangerous, but he also knew less would get done. Garçon looked over to Johnson, but he was not listening to anything the other man was saying. He saw Johnson's mouth moving, but he wasn't hearing anything come out. Garçon then stood up, forcing Johnson to look over to him in an annoyed manner.

"Do you have anything to say?" Johnson asked.

"Yes, I do. Have we accounted for all the nuclear weapons? Once the notion of cleansing becomes widespread, we are going to be dealing with terrorism on a scale that has never been seen before. We have to assume that we are not going to be able to kill off all the individuals who don't pass the standardized tests. And just as with slavery, there are going to be individuals helping these people escape. The anarchists are going to be able to recruit individuals without a problem now."

"What does that have to do with nuclear weapons?" replied Johnson.

"There would be the potential for jihad-type missions carried out by people using nuclear weapons," answered Garçon.

"Garçon, they are trying to escape to stay alive in the first place. Why would they kill themselves by carrying out a terrorist act when they could have just killed themselves by going to war or voluntarily surrendering once they failed the test? I don't think we have anything to worry about, but you bring up a good point. We should be thinking about sharing our inventory of nukes just to be sure," replied Johnson.

Johnson looked up at the group as if he forgot to relay a point but was reminded of it once he began discussing nuclear weapons. "Speaking of nukes, we have devised weapons with the equal power of nuclear weapons. Weapons that are capable of causing substantial damage but with none of the environmental concerns that Japan experienced during the fall out of World War II. Please look at the screen."

The group all turned toward the screen with their full attention. Johnson picked up the remote and pressed the power button. Once the monitor was on, it played footage of the Iraq War in

1992. The label "Top Secret" scrolled across the top of the screen.

"Gentleman and ladies, we never went to war to defend Kuwait in 1992. We went to war to test these bombs on a small scale. As Prime Minister Kan touched upon earlier when he asked about weight proportion, our first projections were off. We thought we could distribute the weight on Earth evenly, so we started to look to the Middle East to colonize. The desert areas are so vast. We felt that defeating Iraq and then Iran via war and establishing our government there was the best way to colonize that land and move people from one area of the world to the desert. We would sustain the land with Operation Storm Cloud and change the weather patterns in the true desert areas to sustain long-term cities and solve the problem that way. We started this by increasing our financial and military backing of Israel and Islam's fights against them as a distraction. Once the Arab world was fixated on the Jews, they wouldn't notice Muslim countries like Dubai and Turkey being increasingly westernized, so we funded Israel's military and Turkey and Dubai's infrastructures. Dubai was one of our magnificent achievements. We knew the Arab world would not let those

54

countries progress without creating a greater threat in their mind to combat, and that was Israel. It is so unfortunate how the threat of Jews and the *white man…*" Johnson said those words with a Native American accent; no one in the room knew if the accent was supposed to be a joke or serious, "working together will get the Islamic extremists so insane they completely take their eyes off the true prize."

Johnson was interrupted by Turkish President Abdullah Sezer. "Mr. President, that must be something that got you many laughs during one of your hillbilly fundraisers, but here, in this room, we just don't get it. So, please continue without the theatrics because there is no need to interrupt your story with ridiculous nonsense again."

All of the other leaders started to smirk, to Johnson's dismay. They were reacting as if Sezer slapped the bully in the playground, but Johnson understood.

Annoyed that his joke didn't receive the response he thought it would, Johnson continued. "We were going to use the war to explain our occupation of the region, but our true mission was to redistribute the world's weight to uninhabitable regions. The process began with Dubai. We supplied the government with the technology to extract sand from the desert and drop it into the sea for land expansion, but once Dubai was fully operational, there was no shift in the orbit, so we decided to switch the mission to extermination. We were hoping Iran would come to Iraq's aid and start a full-scale holy war, with Muslims uniting under Islam, but their differences were too great—" Johnson was interrupted by Brazilian President Fernando Rousseff.

"That is a great idea, Mr. President, but I have two questions," started Rousseff, but Johnson interrupted him before he could continue, for no other reason than to reassert his position in the room. He was clearly still pissed off by the other leaders laughing at him moments prior.

"Your questions are fine, Luiz."

"My name is Fernando," Rousseff replied.

Johnson knew his name, but he said it incorrectly on purpose to prove a point that he was arrogant enough to forget the name of another leader in order to maintain that he was in control of the room. "I apologize…Fernando," replied Johnson. "I would like to answer each question separately, so ask your first question, and I will answer that one and so forth."

Johnson was notorious for doing this during his campaigns. Multiple questions threw him off, so his strategy was to throw off the person asking the question by making him or her separate the questions. He was a master of this because 90 percent of the time, his answer to the first question would be so great that the answer to the second question never mattered.

"No problem, Mr. President. My first question is, why did you abandon it?" asked Rousseff.

"First, we didn't have the support of the world, which is why we stopped after we ended the wars in Afghanistan and Iraq. That much murder and destruction would have ended with the world ready to strike the United States out of fear their nations would be next on the list. We need the support of the world for this operation to work, and as I said before, the projections stated that no matter where the weight was, we were still drifting out of orbit. The only way to put us back on track is by lightening the load and jettisoning weight. What is your next question?"

"The Muslim world would have never gone for colonization of the entire Middle East without a fight. How were you going to get them on board?" responded Rousseff.

"That question is irrelevant now, but our strategy was to gain power through the three Fs," replied Johnson.

"What are the three Fs?" asked Rousseff.

"Force, funds, and food. The people of those regions were so oppressed that the culture dictates following those who show force. Once we took over the region and implemented democracy in Iraq and Iran, we would supply the region with funds. Get the people so dependent on the government by providing a better way of life with improvements on infrastructure that they would embrace change wholeheartedly and without a fight. Personally, I love the idea of war. As a man, this is the only way I can ever replicate the goose bumps I got when I played quarterback in high school and college. Staring down a defense, analyzing the linebackers, and developing a strategy to win—nothing beats that feeling. It's the ultimate rush. But sometimes strategic methods are required. Although we have established the outcome of this war, I am almost happy this happened on my watch. We have a window of four years until the next administration takes over."

"What does the next administration taking over have to do with this?" asked Bennett.

"The next administration may be liberals and their ideology would get in the way of understanding what it takes to complete this mission. During times like this, conservative leadership is needed more than ever because we are not as compassionate as the Democrats we have waiting in the wings. This next generation of Democrats is even more compassionate than Obama ever was, and could you imagine him running this operation?" Johnson said as he looked up to survey the room to see if the others were nodding in agreement. No one showed any changes in emotion, but Bennett was not amused by the Obama reference.

"He was a great president and even has his face on Mount Rushmore, but this is not a mission for a bleeding heart. Look, I am getting off topic. The last F is food. Just as we did with Dubai, we would change the desert area to agricultural and business centers. Farmers and businesspeople would flock to the region, completely forgetting the climate was totally different than any other time in history. You would be surprised at how people begin to question their faith when their bellies are full. Empty stomachs require a savior and a need for religion. Not to mention, people don't join a rebellion against any entity that is feeding them and their families. Once the infrastructure improvements were complete, we would cut back on governmental subsidies and force people to start working for a living and become drones to the new system. You get people working by shaming them off of government assistance. You establish campaigns that turn their neighbors against them, making their neighbors hate them because they feel they are taking care of them with their tax dollars, tax dollars the government is supposed to use to take care of the people anyway. Once that person starts working, the government is generating additional tax dollars, and the cycle continues. We allowed Islam to exist so we could facilitate war. If we wanted to, we could have wiped it from history a long time ago through war and revisionist history. Take a look at slavery in my country. The Blacks in my country practically think those slaves had it easy. Even calling themselves and embracing the word 'nigger,' the very word we used to degrade them. Outside of a couple of movies, we completely changed their mind-sets. If you think we are not capable of doing the same thing with Islam, always remember we are just one war away from that happening." Johnson took a pause to gather himself and reached for a glass of water as if he was on a desert island.

Once he took several deep breaths, he continued. "Speaking of being one war away from being history, we must now decide the ultimate sacrifice: who dies? Who is imprisoned, and whose legacy will be loved and hated?"

A silence came over the room. As different as all the leaders in the room were, they all had one thing in common, the same thing all powerful people have in common: they wanted to live forever and be loved when they die. Even though they all accepted war and the terms of it, no one wanted to sacrifice his or her own life, even if it meant saving the world.

"Everyone, I understand this component is as difficult to accept as any, but know that your fate is not immediate. The war has to end within three years, and war trials can be dragged out for years upon the conclusion of it. There will be none of that George Bush justice where capture means decapitation. You will go before the UN and be judged accordingly," Johnson said in a truly smug voice that stemmed from the laughter from earlier.

"Mr. President, you refer to us as if you are not included," said Yo.

"Of course I am not included. What is wrong with you Yo? Before today, none of you knew about this situation. The United States is going to lose the war, we are going to rebuild your lands and provide you with resources for eternal prosperity, and you still want to kill me. The absolute nerve to even make me a part of the equation is ludicrous. My Department of Defense advisors didn't even want me to tell you about this problem. They suggested we create Category Five hurricanes and tornadoes and destroy entire cities in one shot and blame global warming on the new weather patterns. I advised against that because all nations need to know about this issue, not just the United States, and this is the thanks I get. Now, I don't feel so bad about each nation being included in taking on the expense of creating ships that will transport the mass to space!" screamed Johnson.

"OK, Mr. President, calm down. We get it. But you do realize that your capacity to destroy us must be matched by our own defenses after this is all said and done, right? We can't have our nations subjected to the whims of any madman who takes office after you," said Garçon.

"Nice cleanup, Garçon. I almost thought you were calling me a madman," responded Johnson.

"Not yet…not yet. But we don't know what will happen prior to, during, or after the war. It's been known to break many people, regardless of if we know the outcome or not," said Garçon.

"Everyone, let's understand. Our usage of Operation Storm Cloud is no different than that of a nuclear weapon. I assure you our protocols are no different than the protocols of your nations', especially in regards to the ability to utilize such force. For God's sake, a woman has been president of the United States; you think our forefathers intended for the United States to be a regime and not a democracy? My actions and the actions instituted on behalf of my country are calculated and necessary. Whether it's invading the Middle East or stationing troops in

South Korea, our intentions are never for destruction, only preservation. Operation Storm Cloud's intent was to make unlivable land livable for the sake of humankind. To think of this as being about individual countries is not only selfish, but also small minded." Johnson banged on the table with anger.

"Relax, Johnson," said Wiltshire.

"Don't tell me to relax. Work needs to be done, and we must do it. Now let's get to business and discuss dying, because some of you in this room must go, and it's not going to be me."

Johnson hit a buzzer in the room, and the intercom sounded. "Yes, Mr. President."

"Steve, I think we need a break. We all need some fresh air," replied Johnson.

"Right away, sir," replied Steve.

Johnson released the button and addressed the other leaders in the room. "Ok people, go out and enjoy this day. I think we have done enough for today. Go out on this beautiful land and experience what we are saving. Experience what you will be leaving to your grandchildren and their children. But when you come back, come back with sacrifice on your minds and in your hearts, because this won't get done until sacrifices are made."

The boardroom door opened, and all of the individuals in the room stood up. Everywhere were the sounds of the popping of old knees straightening out and the moans of people with stiff backs and tired muscles who had been sitting in chairs for five hours. Each leader nodded in appreciation to the next man or woman as each of them began to file out of the room. Individual greeters, staff, and personal assistants hurried to meet their assigned leaders as they left the room, so that they could cater to their needs. Johnson's staff were also eyeballing the leaders to nonverbally remind each of them of how important this debriefing was and the need for absolute discretion on this matter.

All of a sudden everyone was startled to hear Wiltshire explode. "I am the prime minister of Great Britain," he bellowed. "Do you really think I need your stares to ensure my discretion?"

Johnson looked outside the room and down the hall to make sure everything was OK, and he realized that Wiltshire had taken issue with the eyeballs he instructed his staff to give each leader as they exited the room. Once he realized that everything was all right and Wiltshire had finally calmed down, he looked over at his chief of staff, Bruce Henderson, and nodded at him with a short smirk. Earlier in the day, before the meeting had started, Johnson had made a bet with Bruce regarding who would be the first to scream that out. Johnson had not thought that debriefing the leaders was even necessary, but Bruce did. So Johnson had compromised with Bruce and allowed the staff to hand out folders with limited information in them. But as each leader took a folder, the staff handing it out would hold on to it tightly to get the leader's attention, look the leader in the eyes, and nod before releasing the folder, giving each leader the unspoken words of discretion.

The idea originated from the Black nanny Johnson had growing up. He had known that he was doing something wrong just by looking at her face, and then he would correct himself. Johnson's parents had given the nanny the right to beat him in their absence if he misbehaved, but the nanny never laid a hand on him. The stare was enough.

Once Johnson gave Bruce the instructions, the two of them bet on who would be the first to break under the pressure, and

Wiltshire was Johnson's first choice. Bruce's choice was Bennett. Despite Johnson's aloof demeanor, the people closest to him knew he had a great ability to read people, so much so that Johnson had gone a step further to say to Bruce that the first person to yell out would also be the first person to volunteer his or her life. Bruce acknowledged Johnson's smirk by nodding at a tilted angle because Johnson was half right, but Bruce then held up his index figure as if to say that President Johnson only had one part of the bet correct so far.

David Wiltshire

As Wiltshire left the meeting and looked towards the White House, he realized how great the day was. The moment overwhelmed him so much that he tilted his head back, closed his eyes, and raised his arms out so that his body looked like a cross in the shadow behind him. Then he took the deepest breath of his life, a breath so deep that he actually started to cough because his lungs were filled with too much oxygen. He opened his eyes. With all the rain lately in Britain, this was the first time in weeks that he had a clear view of the sun, and everything he looked at was even more beautiful than he remembered. He felt a change in his life, as if his objective was to appreciate all the things he had missed and preserve all of the world's wonders for future generations.

When he decided to get into politics, the reasons were different for him than they were now. Coming from a wealthy family, Wiltshire grew up living a life of privilege. His dad was a precious metals mogul, but his business began to suffer during the 1980s as countries began to regulate mining and drilling because of the massive causalities occurring on grounds being unearthed. Faced with the possibility of losing everything,

Wiltshire's dad brought him into his office just days after he had graduated from Oxford.

"Son, you don't know this now, but you will when you become a father. The true measure of a father is whether your children want to follow in your footsteps. We have always been close, but we rarely see eye to eye on a lot of things, so as I've watched you grow into the man you are today, I've conditioned myself to never expect you to follow in my footsteps. Not because you would not want to out of defiance but simply because you have always wanted to create your own path. Making your own way has always been in your personality. Even today, as I look in your eyes, I see you eager to prove you are about to make waves in this world and show me how great you are. And over the years, I've actually used your competitive drive—your desire to win—to make you better. To make us better. I've built you up and made you feel like you could beat me at anything, and then at the last minute I've defeated you, never cheating or allowing you to win. Now look at you today. You're driven and focused. Both of us are ready to reach for the stars, but we got here with different methods." Wiltshire's father held back tears as he spoke.

"Dad, is everything OK? This conversation is weird," Wiltshire replied.

"All is fine, but I am in trouble, son," Wiltshire's father responded.

"What sort of trouble?"

"Business has taken a turn for the worse. We are not getting the contracts we used to anymore. The world is changing, and for us to change with it, I will need you to do something different. Something not on the path you expected to go."

Reluctantly Wiltshire responded, "What's that?"

"I need you to run for public office," his father said.

"Run for office? You know I do not want any part of that, and how can me running for office help with our business problems?" Wiltshire asked.

"Son, we make money from what we are selling to people. But make no mistake; this government controls our business. We used to have unlimited amounts of money to buy the politicians, but with the amount of bribes, on top of mining in locations that didn't pay off, plus our regular business costs, the company's revenues are running close to dry. If you run for office and get elected, that would change everything! You in a position of power, ready to influence legislation and be a foothold in other countries, will save this business. It will save our lifestyle, a lifestyle that your great-grandfather started, and my father and I worked so hard to maintain so you could live a proper life of privilege." Wiltshire's father had a look in his eyes as if he were possessed.

The look on his father's face was one no son should ever see on his father. It was a look of desperation and fatigue. As Wiltshire reminisced about the last time he had seen his father prior to that conversation, he realized that his old man looked as though he aged like an American president. Only stress could bring about that kind of physical change in such a short period of time. Wiltshire knew that running his father's business over the long term was never going to be an option for him, and despite the issues he had with his father putting him in this position, he sincerely loved him.

"Dad, I will do what you need me to do. But how can you ensure I will win?" Wiltshire asked.

"Relax, son. People are robots. Once we get you in front of them, they are going to follow your every word. But once you get in, that's when the real work will begin. Turning around the country through manufacturing and steering them away from technology will be the way I need you to go."

Wiltshire saw the fire in his father's eyes and was nervous to ask him the next question, but he overcame his fear and spoke almost without thinking. "Dad, I went to school to be an engineer. How can I convince the press and the voters that I am trying to lead this country back into the Stone Age with manufacturing all the while going to school for technology?"

"Leadership is as much about acting as it is about making a strong decision. What I am asking you to do now is a temporary solution to save the very way of life you have benefitted from since you were born. What is going to help this company is you getting elected and saving my bum, so your brother and sister can share in the life you had. Look, son, I know we have had our differences in the past, but if you don't want to do this for me, do it for your brother and sister. You have the power to stop the both of them from having their own rooms to sharing one!"

Wiltshire was intrigued by the idea but was equally conflicted because he had been preparing to make his own way his entire life, a way that would set him apart from his family's wealth. His family's wealth had chased him like a monster in a dream. Wiltshire had been constantly running from it but never getting away. In true dream fashion, it had felt like he was running as fast as he could but only moving an inch. It was ironic that the monster he had been running from—the monster that he feared as the most ferocious being in his life—was only running toward him for comfort and not after him to devour him. Ever since he was young he had opposed his father. If his father went left, he went right. If his father wanted red, he got blue. If his father rooted for Liverpool, he rooted for Manchester United, even if his father had bet on Liverpool. It was a practice that had infuriated his father and resulted in Wiltshire's dad labeling him a soccer bad luck charm and never allowing Wiltshire to watch a game with him.

Wiltshire looked at his dad in his eyes, but his dad never maintained eye contact, as if he was ashamed. Wiltshire asked himself, "How dare he ask for help now?"

He had spent years carefully devising a plan to be better, and now his father needed him. But the conflict took a different twist as Wiltshire began to wonder if he should feel vindicated that he was better by default since his father needed his help or if this imaginary rivalry he created was only in his head and not in his father's.

Wiltshire snapped out of his reflection, but he remembered that day vividly, especially after the events of today. It was a day that Wiltshire knew had changed the rest of his life until today. He had accepted his father's plea for help and had run for office, winning in a landslide.

Once he was elected into office, Wiltshire used the influence of the position to gain substantial amounts of governmental contracts and funding for his father's company. The other side of the story was that by saving his father's company, he stalled Britain's technological advances by almost ten years, but he also led England with steady job growth in its manufacturing sector. Because he was intentionally stalling technological advances to help his dad, he overfunded engineering programs throughout the country to ease his guilty conscience. An unexpected benefit of the whole process was that his relationship with his father grew from being competitive to one of a partnership.

Wiltshire utilized the influence and guidance of his father and downright depended on it like a war time general's until his father's death. The two of them were absolutely unstoppable as they outmaneuvered and outsmarted all of Parliament and any opponents who challenged Wiltshire's position. His father's company grew to be one of the largest in the world, and once financial stability was restored, Wiltshire turned the focus back to technology, which caused new job growth in England. The engineering programs he had funded received his full attention, and the advances made were tremendous. Secret projects such as Funnel Fusion were hidden and utilized exclusively by his father's company. The projects were so secret that any scientists involved were transferred to Blake Enterprises and compensated substantially. Any scientists who refused were killed in executions made to look like accidents due to the fear of the technology being leaked.

Blake Enterprises was the only company in the world to utilize Funnel Fusion. It was a process that allowed Blake Enterprises to create gigantic whirlpools in the shape of a funnel from the top of the ocean to the bottom of the ocean floor with gravity propulsion beams. The whirlpools were so deep that one could literally see the bottom of the ocean floor from above in a plane. Once the funnel was created, frost rays would hit the sides of the ocean and freeze them instantly, allowing geologists to climb to the bottom of the ocean floor to actually walk along it to determine if the rock was drillable.

Wiltshire's dad wanted to develop a technology that would prevent poking the ocean floor full of holes to find minerals and thus prevent the weakening of the ocean bed. Research showed that continued mining of the ocean floor was the number one cause of bedrock shifting, which would cause underwater earthquakes and tsunamis. The company also stopped wasting millions of dollars in equipment costs because drilling was useless against certain types of rock located on the ocean floor. The technology was also vital to the company's bottom line because discovering unprofitable mining grounds with actual eyes on the ground instead of on a computer screen hundreds of miles away ended up saving them millions of dollars.

This technology made the subsidiary, Wiltshire Drilling Inc., the richest company in the world because each and every dig was successful. The amount of gold they were able to locate on the ocean floor was beyond measure. Their competitors were invisible because the industry standard for successful to unsuccessful drilling was seven to one, but Wiltshire Drilling's success rate was two to one. It was a ratio that later translated to millions of British pounds pouring into Wiltshire's campaign for prime minister. The advances in technology were without match until his meeting today with the United States.

Until today, Wiltshire had felt that his dad's company would be bigger than any government or any company in the history of the world including Exxon Mobil. What the Americans were capable of, what Johnson demonstrated to his colleagues by controlling the weather from a room hundreds of miles away from the target, made anything that Wiltshire Enterprises could ever imagine almost obsolete.

But these events did not have Wiltshire reminiscing about his past because he was on his deathbed; he was reminiscing about his past to determine if he would sacrifice himself for assassination for the greater good of humanity, history, himself, and his father.

Wiltshire remembered the day his father was dying. He sat in his room with him the whole day, even after the doctors informed him his father had passed away. That day all he could remember was his father talking, laughing, and showing the love every father should share with his son. It was a love that Wiltshire would pass down to his children and generations after. When Wiltshire's son was old enough to understand, he would be able to feel that same love his father had for his grandfather through his dad's words, reflections, expressions, and devotion.

The last day of Wiltshire's dad's life, the old man had imparted some words of wisdom to him. "Life isn't about being rich. Life is about being remembered. Hitler was a scoundrel beyond belief, but I am jealous of him."

When his father said that, Wiltshire's face immediately showed his confusion.

But then his father continued. "Here we are, almost one hundred years later, and the world is still trying to understand him. Through his devious actions, he was the motivation of the entire Jewish faith. Once I die, people will forget about me within a couple of minutes. They will go on with their lives as if I never existed."

"Not to me, Dad," Wiltshire said with complete sincerity.

"I understand, but don't let that happen to you. There will be a time when your life will need to be more than just politics or a company you saved from ruin, more than just being a prime minister, and almost more than being a father. When you get the chance to be remembered a hundred years later, you should not hesitate to take it. Of course, you won't know how you will be remembered, but that won't be important because you'll be dead anyway. Son, I am not saying to go out there and be remembered by killing millions of people, but if your death can motivate generations after yours, you take it. Don't die with regrets like I am about to."

That vision had Wiltshire in such a trance that he felt like his dad was right next to him speaking in his ear. As a spiritual man, Wiltshire felt as if God was giving him a message on what he needed to do when the meeting started back up. This feeling was so overwhelming that he didn't even hear his wife, Joanne, asking him about the meeting.

Outside of his father, Joanne was Wiltshire's most savvy adviser. Never interested in many aspects of politics, Joanne was addicted to the cat-and-mouse tactics of Parliament, the strategy. She was able to read a person from head to toe without that person even saying a word, and she was even better at finding personal weaknesses. Wiltshire knew that lying to her was useless, but based on his outburst from leaving the meeting, he knew that Johnson would either be following him or have him under surveillance.

"Honey, you look like you've seen a ghost. I haven't seen your face like this since the IRA tried to destroy the great Ferris wheel."

Wiltshire wished that the Ferris wheel was his only concern. It would have put people out of the misery they were about to face in the coming months because what was about to happen would be something never seen before.

"Why do you continue to do this to me for every day of our marriage and eighty-five percent of the time when we were dating?"

Joanne knew exactly what Wiltshire was referring to, but she played coy about it anyway. She responded smugly, "What do you mean, my dear? I have no clue what you're talking about. Besides, why do you try to withhold things from me anyway? You do know I have ways of getting the information that I want." She opened her legs, revealing she wasn't wearing any panties.

"Please, Jo. I've seen that for so many years, it doesn't work on me anymore," he smiled.

"That's true, but today…today it tastes different," Joanne said seductively.

"Not today, tiger. The less you know, the better. But, just so that you know, this is worse than the IRA by miles," said Wiltshire.

"OK, Churchie (the nickname Joanne gave him after Winston Churchill). Let's get some dinner, OK? We are in the land of the free and the home of the brave, so let's be both," said Joanne.

"Are you asking me if I will go on a date with you tonight?" asked Wiltshire.

"Of course, my love," replied Joanne as she uncrossed and recrossed her legs in a sexual manner.

Joanne was stunned that her husband wasn't blabbing about what the meeting was about, but that wasn't the issue for her. The issue was she wasn't part of the solution. Billed by the British press as the Hillary Clinton of Downing Street, knowing the information wasn't necessary for Joanne, but being the brains behind the solution while the other parties were thinking they came up with the solution was. Joanne married Wiltshire not because he wasn't great at hiding things or tremendously good looking; she married him because he was the closest man who could match her drive and intellect. What she didn't know was that Wiltshire knew he could never match her intellect because Joanne was just too cunning and strategic, but he was a master at making her believe that he could.

Prior to meeting Wiltshire, Joanne had never had a shortage of suitors, all of whom were wealthy and fully capable of providing for her every need. But when she met Wiltshire, she knew he was the one because he was adaptable. In Joanne's eyes, there was nothing worse than a man who knew she was smarter than him but who was so competitive that he would minimize her talents and abilities instead of using them to make them both better as a unit and not as individuals.

As she looked at Wiltshire now, at all the worry in his face, she began to reflect on their first argument and how he ended it.

"You think I don't know you are testing me, Joanne?" Wiltshire yelled at her. "Why play this game with me, because I will never win. You were born to read people as if you are playing a game of chess, so I am dropping my king. You win! Now, what are you going to do? Keep going? Or are we going to find a way to mix our genes and put them into some offspring, so our children can rule this planet?"

No one ever knew the story, but that very night Joanne did what few women ever did. She asked Wiltshire to marry her.

"What do you think this is?" asked Wiltshire.

"What do you mean? Will you marry me, you wanker?" Joanne replied with the same stunned looked every man had on his face when she told him "no" after he asked for her hand in marriage.

"How can you ask me to marry you when you don't have a ring to give me? What do you think I am, a desperate floozy who would say 'yes' without a ring? Besides, you didn't even ask my dad for my hand in marriage. Geez. Now, get off your knee, and let's get some dinner," Wiltshire responded in a playful yet serious manner.

Over the years, they would reflect on that story and laugh about it while making the phrase "Let's get some dinner" their secret code for talking about an issue later or sitting down together to work out a course of action for Wiltshire's political dealings.

As the two were in the limo, Wiltshire begin to stare out of the window with his right arm leaning on the arm rest and his chin firmly pressed between his thumb and index finger. He had already made up his mind that he would sacrifice himself to provide rationale for England to enter the war, but preparing his family was going to be the major obstacle.

The limo waited in traffic, and the ride made Wiltshire's decision much clearer. His family had more money than it could ever spend in three lifetimes, and Joanne, who truly loved Wiltshire, would flourish with the attention she would get from the tragedy. Wiltshire's son, William, was old enough to know his father, and Wiltshire would still be his hero, but he was young enough to be taught to recognize his father's heroism.

The one aspect Wiltshire was nervous about was if he could trust Johnson to keep his word. This "new earth" that was about to commence didn't ensure that money was going to be valued the same way, so Wiltshire had to ensure that if Johnson and the others accepted his sacrifice, once he was gone, the world wouldn't paint him as anything negative, causing his wealth to be devalued based on public perception or, even worse, the pound no longer being recognized resulting in Joanne being broke and the world blaming her for whatever story Johnson and the others concocted.

The idea was highly unlikely, but he never trusted the Americans after reading how falsely they went to war in Iraq. As his paranoid thoughts continued to engulf him, he began to think about securing enough gold and diamonds to ensure the viability of Wiltshire Enterprises once this process began. To the outside world, Wiltshire Enterprises was a drilling company looking for minerals, but to a certain subgroup within the company, it was an organized group of pirates and treasure hunters.

Once the Funnel Fusion had been perfected, Wiltshire began to research Britain's historical record for shipping routes utilized since the establishment of the empire. Companies had been researching these routes for years but had been unable to reach the bottom of the ocean floor due to the pressure of deep-sea diving. But with the Funnel Fusion, Wiltshire Enterprises had the ability to reach the depths so once the shipwrecks were located, they were able to loot the treasures and priceless artifacts. While one team was looking for lost treasures, another team was analyzing the rock and locating vast amounts of gold located within the rock underneath the sea.

These ventures resulted in Wiltshire Enterprises establishing a secret fort and storing all of the resources near the island of Madagascar. The fort was guarded by electronically controlled robots that Wiltshire had engineered himself during his engineering days at Oxford.

The robots were engineered to protect anyone with Wiltshire's family DNA. His family's medical records were constantly being updated so no army could hurt them once they were at the fort. Plus, if anyone were able to overrun the robots, all the treasure within the fort would be locked away in a self-enclosed tunnel that would be impossible to open. Wiltshire had designed this preventive measure after watching a National Geographic special on how the physical US Constitution is preserved should the United States be invaded and the government overrun.

With the resources there for Joanne, the only component left to chance was if Johnson and the others decided to vilify him. How would Joanne get access to the fort, especially with the world watching her every move after his death and with a new world order being implemented?

The car finally arrived to the restaurant when Wiltshire's phone rang.

"Hello?" answered Wiltshire.

"Is this a secured line?" asked the voice on the other end in an Asian accent.

"This is a secured line."

"Please state your secured line access code. Once the code is given, all other radio transmissions and communication will be disconnected, and only this phone will be operational. Please clear a three-foot radius before you are connected."

"Is everything OK, honey?" asked Joanne.

"Yes, everything is fine. Please go ahead into the restaurant, and I will meet you in there."

Joanne leaned over and gave Wiltshire a kiss before getting out of the car.

"Driver, I need privacy," stated Wiltshire in a firm manner.

The driver exited the limo. Two armed security guards escorted Joanne into the restaurant. The security personnel assigned to protect Wiltshire remained outside the car.

"All clear. The security code is 060922SSK," said Wiltshire.

"All clear," said the voice on the other end of the phone.

The new phone system had been implemented so that world leaders could communicate directly to each other. Each nation had appointed technology personnel to develop a secure line with translators who had been vetted and personally appointed to operate the lines. The phone system was created to prevent nuclear war after several Mexican cartels joined forces to gain access to nuclear weapons and threatened the United States with detonation if it did not allow the cartel's drugs to cross the borders unchecked. It was the closest the world had come to nuclear war since the Cuban missile crisis.

The phone system had been installed because the Mexican drug cartels had purchased and launched satellites and were using them to destroy government-owned satellites. Communications had been cut, and there was limited correspondence between countries at that time, which resulted in all countries readying their nuclear weapons for attack because they did not know the Mexican cartels were in control. The cartels had been able to hack into the limited available systems to access any communications that would be used to develop a plan to fight the cartels.

For three months, the United States had been forced to allow drugs to come into the country freely. But in the end, the drug cartels had been defeated because of communications via Morse code. Each country's leader had ordered the destruction of all satellites except for one, so they could track where the cartels were hiding out. The weapons had been found in storage containers in three separate locations: Turkey, Hong Kong, and Florida. The cartels were eliminated, and all new satellites were launched with force fields protecting them. The process cost billions of dollars because private sector satellites were forced to relaunch and comply with the new technology.

The current system had two specific components for the world leaders. Communications were either individual conversations or conference calls. After the crisis, international law stated that if the communication had more than three leaders on the call, all the leaders associated with the call would have to agree to the conversation being taped. If the communication had three or less leaders, the conversation only required their personalized security clearance code and their interpreters on the line.

"Security clearance accepted. Prime Minister Yo has waived his interpreter and will speak to you directly. You may begin speaking," said the voice on the line.

"It has been a long time, my friend. I had a feeling you would be calling me today," said Wiltshire.

"Yes, it has. Your father was a great man, and you have not fallen far from the tree," replied Yo.

"Thank you, Emperor, but to what do I owe this phone call?"

"I just wanted to touch base with you. I heard your outburst as we were leaving the meeting, and I can imagine how stressful this is for you."

Wiltshire was puzzled by Yo singling him out as if Yo himself wasn't stressed by the meeting as well. "I hardly believe I was the only one stressed by today's meeting. Granted, I should not have yelled out like that, but we were discussing the lives of billions of people. Our way of life is going to be completely changed from this day forward." Wiltshire attempted to hold back his anger.

"Death is a part of life. We are in this position because we have managed to skip dying well past the time we were supposed to. I have dreamt of this day for so long, and I am ready for what this new day—or new life—will bring. War without the threat of nuclear weapons is a powerful rush for me. With this plan, we will see whose strategy is better, whose armies are stronger, or who can win," Yo said with enthusiasm.

"Yo, how can you feel this way when the fight is fixed? We all know what the outcome is going to be."

"This is true, but when we reconvene, I will request that the battle for one region will go unfixed. China versus America for the island of Madagascar," said Yo.

"Why Madagascar?" asked Wiltshire. He wondered if Yo was trying to discreetly say something, since Wiltshire's gold reserve was located near that country.

"Because the land mass does not give an advantage to either China or America. Based on the location, our strategy, military might, and ability to provide resources for our troops and weaponry will dictate the winner. We have been trying to find a way to prove we are better than the Americans for centuries. For decades, my people have fled my country to go to America, each of them thinking that it's better there than in China. It has always been my mission to prove to my people that we are the greatest nation in the world, so we set out to prove it by buying all their debt and controlling their economy. We achieved this, and yet my people still want to go there. We will use the media to communicate to the world the importance of this battle and that the winner will control the tide of the war. Obviously, if the Americans win, we will use the media to say another battle will turn the tide. People will believe anything they are told. Once we win this fake war, they will stay, but in my mind I will know if we were better or not. How can we ever test my army if we never use it under normal battle conditions? The fight for Madagascar will show us who is best."

Wiltshire was conflicted by what he was hearing from Yo. This whole time he had been trying to figure out if he would sacrifice his life for the greater good of humanity, so to hear his friend revel in the possibility of death and destruction was disturbing to him. Wiltshire no longer wanted to listen to Yo, so he decided to cut the conversation short and consider how to further protect his gold from Yo should the room go with him on his request.

"Yo, let me go. Tonight will be one of the few times I will be able to have dinner with Joanne, and I don't want miss it by discussing the same things that almost made me vomit earlier."

"Oh no, Wiltshire. I don't want to hold you back from Joanne. How is she doing these days?"

"She is doing well. Furious I won't tell her what we discussed today, but I don't want to make her even angrier by keeping her waiting for dinner."

"Yes, yes. Please go, and we will talk tomorrow."

Wiltshire hung up the phone quickly, thinking how lucky Perez was that he didn't have to deal with any of this now.

Jiang Yo

Yo handed the phone to an advisor and asked him, "Can you fix me a drink, Chao?"

"No problem, sir. What would you like?" replied Chao as he bowed his head to acknowledge the request.

"Give me a brandy with no ice. And will the American women be ready?"

"Yes, they will be here shortly," replied Chao as he went to the liquor cabinet to fix Yo a drink.

"As a matter of fact, please fill the cup. I want to get drunk tonight. I have never had sex with an American woman in America, and I am ready to see how it feels. After all, tonight is a celebration. After today, life as we know it will never be the same," said Yo joyously.

"Why do you say that, sir?"

"That I cannot tell you, but rest assured that you will be kept safe by my side."

As Yo talked, he began to stare deeply at Chao. He was reflecting on the day Chao was born, but his deep reflection didn't stop there. He began to reminisce far back into his life, to when he was a young man and how close he too came to death, but unlike Perez he lived to be in that meeting today.

Knowing that his whole life had been planned for him because of his parents, Yo had always longed for three things: combat; pure competition in every phase of his life with no one giving him a break because of his position in life; and unconditional acceptance from his people.

The thirst for those three components made him decide to train with the Chinese secret force, the People's Liberation Army. He read about Prince William going to Afghanistan in 2010 and was inspired to follow in his footsteps to one day fight for China in a great war of his own. As time passed and China's economic power outgrew its military might, Yo realized that fighting alongside this secret forces unit was becoming less and less likely.

One day during his training, his frustrations overwhelmed him, and he challenged Feng Lin, the best fighter in the entire camp, to a fight. He ordered Lin to fight without holding back, as if he were fighting against the man who had murdered his son. Lin immediately attacked him, throwing several combinations of kicks and punches that Yo easily blocked and countered with a right cross that nearly ended the fight.

Since Lin was the best fighter in the class, Yo's confidence began to swell as Lin began to tire, but Lin did not want to leave Yo with the impression he was throwing the fight even though Yo was clearly beating him. Most people don't know that when a fighter is clearly overmatched, he will lose the battle in his mind first, resulting in an overwhelming feeling of loss. This feeling can overtake a man who is getting beat.

Lin made up in his mind that his next combination would be his last before he started to conserve energy to dodge Yo the rest of the fight. Lin faked a leg sweep, resulting in Yo jumping to avoid the hit. As Yo jumped up, Lin stood up straight. While Yo was in the air, Lin kicked him in the thigh. The force from the hit was so hard that it broke a blood vessel in Yo's leg. Yo immediately went down in pain as the medics rushed toward him. Both of the doctors tried to get Yo to straighten out his body out so that they could look at the wound. Once they did, they saw the blood pooling underneath his skin.

Yo continued to be macho by not screaming out even though the pain was unbearable. As the medics took him to the medical facility on the base, they prepared for an emergency operation. Yo requested that he remain awake during the operation, and the surgeons granted his request.

As they began to operate, the doctors noticed that not only was the blood vessel in his leg broken but the kick was so close to his groin that the vessel that produces sperm was heavily damaged as well.

Yo noticed the surgeon's face and asked him, "What, doctor? What do you see? Please tell me!"

The doctor was hesitant and unsure how to answer because he feared for his life and how Yo would react. But he overcame his fear and gave Yo the gruesome news.

"Yo, your prostate vessel was heavily damaged, and it's beyond repair. Once this surgery is complete, you will not be able to produce any sperm, so fathering a child will be almost impossible."

The news immediately devastated Yo, but the doctor continued. "I do see that a substantial amount of sperm exists now. I am asking for your permission to extract the remaining sperm you have, so we can save it for you should you decide to use it in the future."

Yo did not respond with words, but he nodded in approval.

"Since the blood has mixed with the remaining sperm, I am not sure if it will be usable, but we will do everything we can to save as much of it as possible."

Yo was relieved and said, "Please extract the remaining sperm first, and then complete the operation. Once the extraction is complete, I am requesting that the remaining operation be performed with me asleep. I fear that I will lose my leg, and I don't want to know about that or put you in the position to try to save it or lose your life. Today, my heart aches as if there has been a great death in my life, and I don't wish to make a decision that will cause a death in yours. Please continue and do what you must do going forward."

The doctor nodded his head in approval and granted Yo's request by putting him to sleep for the remainder of the surgery.

Yo now looked at Chao deeply because Chao was unaware that he was actually engineered because of orders issued by Yo, his father. It was now eighteen years since that incident, and Chao was the son Yo had always longed for, but his thirst to be number one would not allow him to tell Chao this information.

Unable to have children the conventional way, Yo set out for constant approval from the people of China. Despite his position and power, Yo was truly a calculating man. Even though he had sent people to death in the past, his decision to do so was always strategic. Individuals of intelligence and contributors to society were never sent to death. His philosophy had always been, why kill someone who can contribute to the greater good of humankind when you can send the same message by killing a lesser individual? He usually executed others of reduced intellect and ability but only to prove a point, and his point was to demonstrate that he was a man of decisive action.

Yo maintained a diary on all of the individuals around him. He knew everything about the men and women in his inner circle and ranked them according to usefulness. But on that operating table eighteen years ago, he was powerless and at the mercy of the surgeons. The surgeons were so paranoid that despite their thoughts to intentionally botch the surgery, each of them was fearful Yo had a contingency plan.

Once the surgery was completed, the chief surgeon gave him the horrific news.

"Your Excellency, this amount of sperm was all I could save," he said as he raised a tube containing about a teaspoon of liquid. "But we cannot afford to wait by freezing it for later use. Since a substantial amount of blood has mixed with the sperm, we must find a female to impregnate immediately. Do you have anyone in mind? Please know it will be best if we extract an egg from the female to ensure fertilization. More conventional methods may prove unsuccessful. Please think it over, sir," the doctor concluded.

Yo felt sick to his stomach. All he could do was think about the error in judgment he had made during the fight. Underestimating his opponent had been a huge error, and what compounded the situation was that he didn't know of any potential mothers. As his drive for perfection and competition had taken over his life, he had completely neglected his personal life; training and fighting were his passions. He had not encountered any women to whom he would be able to say, "Be the mother to my child." The women he knew wouldn't say no because they were not interested but rather because they didn't know him, and he knew nothing about them. But what he did have were the rankings of his inner circle.

He immediately summoned a nurse to carry out his instructions as he lay in the bed. "Nurse, please contact this number and ask for Bo Chung right away."

The nurse complied with Yo's request, and within twenty minutes he was by Yo's side. Chung was Yo's most trusted advisor, and once Yo had informed him of his dilemma, Chung immediately began to help him evaluate potential candidates.

As the two sat going through all the backgrounds of the women, Yo broke the tension by making a joke. "I wish Mitt Romney were here, because he would be able to give us binders of women. Then this wouldn't be a problem."

He was referencing what Romney had said during his debate with Obama during the 2012 election. The two laughed as they reflected on watching that debate together on YouTube.

Finally, after hours of looking at the file, the search came down to two women: Ah Lam Lee, who was married, and Lifen Wong, who was not.

Yo was an honorable man, so placing a married woman in this position was a last resort. He instructed Chung to summon Lifen Wong to the hospital. Chung immediately left to bring her before Yo. Lifen was not only beautiful but also a true intellectual. Yo had secretly observed her movements before, and she had caught him looking at her on more than one occasion. Her specialty in Yo's cabinet was military strategy, but she was actually a scientist at the forefront of finding a cure for the H1N1 virus.

Chung arrived at Lifen's apartment, and to his surprise he saw that she had company with her. A male guest. Chung, a master at reading body language and analyzing individuals, observed the interaction between the two after Lifen invited him into her home.

"Lifen please forgive me for interrupting you tonight, but it is very urgent. I am sure you are aware of Yo's condition," said Chung.

"I am. My assistant called just before you arrived and told me. Will he be OK?"

"Yes, he will. But can we talk in private to discuss the next bit of information I have for you? It is classified."

"Of course. Walk this way."

Chung was amazed at how nice Lifen's house was as he walked down the hallway. The abstract artwork hanging on the walls and throughout the house caught Chung's attention because the works were extraordinary and Lifen was so structured while on duty. He would have never guessed her taste in artwork based on her professional life. She laughed.

"Why are you laughing?" Chung asked.

"I was wondering if he sent you to fulfill the wish of a dying man or if you are shocked by my paintings."

"You are only half right. I am shocked by the paintings, but he isn't actually dying, but there is an issue." As Chung began to debrief Lifen, her face turned from smiling to complete dismay and amazement. She didn't know how to tell Chung that the man downstairs had just proposed to her two days ago, but she knew she must.

"Chung, your timing couldn't be more terrible. Dun asked me to marry him two days ago. I didn't wear my ring to work because I was not sure if I was willing to accept his offer. I thought about it for two days and literally just accepted. That is why he is downstairs."

"Well, I am not sure that he even has to know. Yo just wants an egg. We do hope you can carry the baby, but that is not mandatory since finding a surrogate would be fairly easy. But, keep in mind, you said yourself you weren't sure if you even wanted to marry him."

"I understand, but since I accepted, I have no choice but to let him know. I will do it, but he must be informed. Can I speak honestly?"

"Of course you can."

"It's not like I have much of a choice in this matter, do I?"

Chung's face was filled with apprehension as he anticipated what Lifen was about to say next. Lifen observed Chung's facial expression and immediately became hesitant.

"You know how Yo is. If he finds out that I snuck behind my fiancée's back, he will assume I am not trustworthy, and that will be the end of my career."

Lifen was actually terrified that if she didn't have the child, Yo would kill her anyway, so the amount of pressure she was under was tremendous.

"I understand, and that makes total sense, but I need you to listen, Lifen. There is one more stipulation. The amount of sperm Yo has left is severely limited. Because so much blood mixed with the sperm, the doctors were not able to save most of it. Artificial insemination is the only way for the egg to be fertilized, and that method is not guaranteed, which is why you may not need to tell him anything pertaining to this conversation. The doctor won't even freeze the sperm because he fears the whole sample could be lost."

"I extend to you Yo's deepest and sincerest appreciation for putting you into this situation, but due to the timing, we have a car outside and will need to take you to the facility right away," said Chung.

"Let me get my things together, and give me a little extra time to tell my fiancée about what I have decided to do."

Chung bowed his head and left the room, but as he walked through the living room, he saw that Dun was not sitting down anymore. Chung turned the corner and saw Dun chopping onions for a broth he had been stewing on the stove. Chung walked over to him and bowed his head to him to denote his departure.

As Chung left, Lifen entered the kitchen with a concerned look on her face.

"What is wrong, Lifen?" asked Dun.

"Nothing is wrong, but if you are to be my husband, outside of my job, I do not wish to keep anything from you."

"Thank you, but what is the matter?"

"The emperor's son, Yo, was badly injured, and he has requested that I give him one of my eggs to artificially inseminate so that he can have a child."

Dun's face immediately filled with despair because his love for Lifen was blinding, and as long as the two had known each other, Lifen was completely unaware of how jealous Dun was.

He began to chop the onions more aggressively and asked, "Will this request require you to have sex with him?"

"No. They will only extract the egg, and it will be artificially inseminated. The procedure will be fast and painless."

"Who will carry the baby?" asked Dun.

"Commander Chung is the man who just left. I will find out that information once I see him shortly. In fact, I sincerely believe that the less you know, the better."

"Were there any other women he could have asked?"

"I am not sure if there were any other women based on the information that Commander Chung gave me, but Yo was tremendously isolated, so there may not be many others. He takes marriage and commitments very seriously."

"So, if you had accepted my proposal three days ago, then you would have been out of contention as well, right?" asked Dun.

"That is a question I cannot answer. But I am not sure how it is relevant, because even if I did say yes right away, we would still not be married today."

Dun resumed cutting the onions, but his emotions did not let him realize the onions were minced so fine, it was as if they were cut by a blender. Lifen also noticed that Dun narrowly missed cutting his fingers many times.

Being a tremendous judge of character, Lifen decided it was best to remove herself from the kitchen and call in Commander Chung for protection. So that Lifen would not arouse Dun's suspicion, she took her right hand and gently placed it on top of Dun's left hand to reassure him and to prevent him from chopping off his fingers.

He looked down and was embarrassed by the amount of chopping he had done. Lifen took the onions and the cutting board and placed them directly over the boiling pot and put the onions in the broth.

She placed her hand on his cheek and said, "Continue the broth, my love. I will be back shortly, and we will eat it together when I get back."

Lifen went toward the door where she saw Commander Chung.

"Why are you standing outside? It's so cold. Come inside until I am ready."

Chung bowed his head in acceptance and entered the house and stood in the foyer. He was completely unaware that Lifen invited him in because she was nervous about Dun's behavior.

"Wait here. I will be right down," said Lifen as she left the foyer area and went upstairs to gather some clothing.

Dun noticed Commander Chung standing at the door. The two did not acknowledge each other's presence until they both looked up at Lifen coming downstairs with a bag in her hand.

Lifen looked at Dun as she came close to him to kiss him good-bye. Due to the angle Dun was standing against the wall, no one noticed he had the knife in his hand. Dun embraced Lifen with a light kiss and hug. As she began to turn toward the door to leave, Dun pulled her arm back, causing her whole body to turn around until both of them were face-to-face.

"I am sorry, Lifen," he said. "But I will not share you or any part of you with anyone else. If I am not the first man to father your children, no one will be." He then plunged the knife into Lifen's stomach.

Lifen immediately fell to the ground and went into the fetal position, holding the wound as blood poured from her body and onto the floor. Dun then turned to Chung, who stood frozen and in shock by Dun's actions. Dun shifted the bloody knife to his right hand, which was his more powerful hand, and ran toward Chung with the knife raised above his head.

Chung attempted to remove his gun from his holster, but the trigger of the gun got struck in the holster flap.

By the time Chung realized that removing the gun in time to shoot Dun was impossible, he saw Dun was just a few feet away, ready to stab him. Chung's only defense was to raise his left forearm to prevent himself from being stabbed in the head. The knife came down through Chung's forearm, leaving Dun's midsection open to counter.

Chung twisted his forearm, forcing Dun to lose his grip on the knife, and Chung then punched Dun in the stomach with his free hand. Dun immediately buckled in agony, giving Chung a chance to remove his gun from its holster. With the knife stuck in his forearm and his weapon removed, Chung walked toward Dun and shot him twice in the head.

As he called for help and opened the door, he realized that Lifen was still breathing. He ran over to her and saw she was trying to say something. With his right ear nearly touching Lifen's lips, he could barely make out her words.

"Get me to the hospital. Don't worry about saving me. Perform the procedure, so you can save the egg for Yo."

Without wasting time and totally disregarding the knife sticking in his forearm, Chung picked up Lifen and carried her to the car as they both continued to lose substantial amounts of blood.

Lifen's body was totally sapped of energy. She lay motionless on the car seat. Chung's facial expression was emotionless, as his adrenaline did not allow him to feel the pain of having a knife stuck in his forearm. He was completely focused on getting Lifen to the hospital to fulfill Yo's request to get the egg and to save her life.

Lifen's house was just a straight drive to the hospital, but the driver decided to take the back roads because they were usually clear of traffic at night.

Calling ahead, the driver was able to obtain an escort of officers to make sure their arrival was expedient. Chung's adrenaline began to wear off, and he started to feel the pain of the stab wound. The blood seeping from Lifen's wound was uncontrollable, and the journey to the hospital, although relatively short, seemed like it was taking forever for both of them.

"Wow, this has been quite a day," said Lifen as she struggled to get the words out loud enough for Chung to hear and break the tension in the car.

Chung had to smile as he responded, "True indeed. You sure know how to pick them."

"The truth is, I knew something was off about him, which is why it took so long for me to say yes, but I didn't imagine him doing something like this," said Lifen as she grimaced with pain.

"For some reason women never anticipate these reactions in the men they are with, but love is crazy. It will make you do some insane things," said Chung.

The divider in the car then came down, and the driver said, "General Chung, I have received confirmation that the hospital is ready for you. As soon as we get there, the medical staff will be right there for you and Inspector Lifen."

Chung was trying to conserve his energy, but he responded by saying, "Please inform them to take Inspector Lifen first and then me."

The driver nodded his head in agreement and raised the divider to focus on driving.

"General?" said Lifen.

"Stop talking, Lifen. Please conserve your energy," said Chung.

"I understand, sir, but please notify the medical personnel that they are to save the egg for Prime Minister Yo and attempt to save my life as a secondary measure. I am not sure I will be able to survive this."

"Lifen, please don't think like that. You are going to be fine!" replied Chung. Chung knew that her egg was the priority, but looking at Lifen lying on the car seat bleeding uncontrollably, he would never have said that.

The car pulled into the facility's entrance, and Chung could see that hospital personnel were there waiting. A doctor opened the car door while the tires were still in motion. Lifen was pulled out of the car, placed on a stretcher, and rushed into the entrance.

Chung was able to get out of the car on his own and was then placed in a wheelchair. He looked back inside the car and was able to see how much blood had pooled on the floor. He looked at it in amazement, wondering to himself how two people could lose so much blood and still be alive.

Chung had held out for as long as he could but began to fade in and out of consciousness as he was wheeled into the hospital. The blood loss was finally taking a toll on him, and the realization that he was about to die was finally dawning on him.

The doctor walking alongside Chung's wheelchair said to him, "You are lucky you left the knife in your forearm. Most people usually take the object out of their body, not realizing the object sometime acts as a stopper to clog the hole. The knife appears to be near an artery, so we must stop the bleeding as soon as possible. Why didn't you tie something above the wound to prevent blood loss? Aren't you soldiers supposed to be trained in this sort of thing?"

Chung was embarrassed by what the doctor said, first because what he said was true. He thought to himself, "How could I not think to reduce the circulation by tying something above the wound?" Second, he was embarrassed because the doctor said that in front of people. Chung was a hard-nosed soldier, and if anyone knew that he was unable to defend himself because he couldn't take his gun out of his holster, he would be a laughingstock. The thought alone got Chung so mad that he took out his gun and shot the doctor in the foot. The sound from the gun startled everyone in sight. The doctor fell down immediately in agony.

"Are you crazy? What the hell did you do that for?" screamed the doctor.

Chung responded, "Stop crying. It's only a flesh wound. If I wanted to be cruel, I would have shot you in the hands so you could never work again."

"That doesn't explain why you shot me, you lunatic!" the doctor shouted.

"It's simple. Aren't you doctors supposed to know what to do in times like these? I just wanted to make sure," replied Chung.

Chung's military status and relationship to Yo pretty much guaranteed that no consequences would come from his actions, but Chung's senses then kicked in, letting him know that nothing good was going to come from his actions. And he was correct; his actions forced the hospital to send in a doctor with limited experience to perform his surgery. China already had a limited number of doctors. Chung did not know it, but his new doctor had performed five surgeries earlier in the day, and two of the patients had died.

Chung's fate had basically been sealed by his actions, but he was a prideful man and would never admit it, so instead he signaled for the nurse. She immediately came over.

"I have a couple of requests. Please get a pen and paper to write them down," said Chung.

"I have a pretty good memory, sir. You can just tell them to me, and I will remember," responded the nurse.

Chung was truly annoyed, but his previous actions with the doctor required him to contain his emotions. "Nurse, I would appreciate if you would humor me by writing down what I am about to say, so please get a pen and paper."

The nurse rushed to get the pen and paper to fulfill Chung's request. "I'm sorry, sir. Please go ahead."

"First, please let the administrators know how important saving Lifen is to Emperor Yo. Second, her egg is to take precedent over her life. Please extract the egg first and then perform the procedure to save her life. Third, contact my sister and inform her that her brother requests that she be the surrogate for Yo's baby." Chung then told the nurse his sister's address.

Chung's request to have his sister carry Yo's baby would ensure that the family would be taken care of if he did not survive. He had no children of his own due to his devotion to Yo, so his sister, who was fourteen years younger than Chung, had been like a daughter to him since their father died while on a military training mission when she was just a baby.

"Fourth, tell my wife I love her. Finally, do not let Yo know about what happened tonight with Lifen and me. If something happens to her during surgery, please tell Yo that she died due to complications with the procedure. His head must be clear to run this country, and I do not wish for him to have to look at his child's face and reflect on what happened today."

The nurse responded, "Wow that was a lot. I am glad you did tell me to get a pen, because that was a lot to remember." The nurse was actually being sarcastic because she did remember every word he said, but she felt that not trying to comfort or fulfill every wish of someone in Chung's position would be cruel. She bowed her head in acceptance and left the room to inform her colleagues.

She walked into Lifen's room so she could see what was going on. She noticed that Lifen was still alive, but no one was in the room with her.

"Where is everyone? This women needs medical attention," the nurse yelled out.

As she began rushing out of the room, a team of surgeons rushed in, nearly trampling her.

"Why did you leave her in this room alone with her surgery not being completed?" asked the nurse.

"There was an issue with Emperor Yo, and we were pulled away to tend to him. The issue was resolved, so we rushed back here," said the lead surgeon.

The nurse did not believe the doctor, but she accepted his response and chose not to question him further.

"Please leave this room now! You are not authorized to be here," said the surgeon in an angry tone.

The nurse complied and left the room. One of her colleagues was just outside the door.

"What going on?" asked the other nurse.

"Emperor Yo has requested her egg because he had a horrible training accident that left him sterile. Once we extract the egg, the doctor wanted to deliver it personally to the emperor so that they can have it fertilized. The doctor didn't want anyone in the room until he got back," stated the nurse.

"He told me to monitor her condition and heart rate while he was gone, and I honored his request. They removed the egg and sent it for embryonic fertilization. We don't know who the surrogate mother is though," stated the second nurse.

"I know who she is. General Chung instructed me to have you call his sister because she is supposed to be the surrogate. Here is her information," she replied.

The first nurse handed the second nurse the note, and the second nurse immediately sent for military personnel to bring Chung's sister to the hospital.

"There is no time to lose," she instructed the soldiers. "Emperor Yo's sperm has very little time left. You are to go to this address and bring her to me at once. Do not let her pack a bag or even go to the bathroom. Nothing! Pick her up and bring her directly here. Your one and only objective is bringing her to this hospital as soon as possible."

The soldiers left immediately.

The nurse who Chung had given the message to went back to the operating room to observe the procedure through the window. As she neared the room, she began to hear a lot of commotion. Once she was in front of the observation window, she saw the doctors performing emergency procedures to revive Lifen. As she witnessed this, she placed both of her hands flat on the window as if she was trying to hold up the wall with all her strength.

Her emotions began to overwhelm her. She knew that if only the doctors had stayed in the room instead of leaving her there, Lifen wouldn't be having CPR performed on her. The nurse's face turned red with emotion, and she screamed out in disgust as the doctors decided to discontinue trying to bring Lifen back to life. The nurse's scream could be heard by everyone in the hospital except those in the operating room. Since the hospital was a teaching hospital, the operating rooms were soundproof to ensure that no one in the room would be distracted while performing surgery.

As the doctors left the room, the nurse confronted them angrily. "If you didn't stop the operation and leave her in this room, this wouldn't have happened. Now a woman is dead because of your negligence."

The doctor replied, "I know you are upset, but some lives are just more important than others."

What that doctor didn't know was that Lifen was the nurse's sister. The nurse had no idea her sister was in the hospital until she went into Lifen's room. When she realized the patient was her sister, she went to look for the medical personnel to ask why they left her alone in the first place.

Due to the security protocols implemented by Yo where family members must be kept secret to prevent intelligence risks, the nurse was powerless to use her position in the hospital as collateral for special treatment.

The nurse began looking for a place to discreetly mourn, out of the sight of others. She rushed to a back staircase and immediately placed her back on the wall. Her emotion was so great that she couldn't hold herself upright, and she slid down to a seated position and buried her head between her knees. As she began to regain her composure, she heard her name being called out on the loudspeaker. She rushed to the nearest bathroom to wipe her face and then hurried out to the front desk. Once she arrived at the desk, she saw the hospital administrators waiting for her.

"General Chung has died. We are in contact with his sister, and she is on her way, but we don't want you to tell her about his death until the procedure is done. Her stress may cause her body to reject the impregnated egg, and the emperor's chances of having a child will be lost. Since you are the one he spoke with before he died, we would like for you to tell her Yo's instructions. Once she accepts them, we are offering you the chance to be in the operating room to assist with the surgery."

The nurse, still mourning her sister's death, got up enough energy to nod her head in agreement. She was conflicted. The baby would be her sister's, but it would be given to a man who told the hospital staff to save her egg rather than her life. She had no clue of Yo's true feelings for Lifen and how he genuinely admired her from afar. His sense of honor in selecting her was a true source of conflict for Yo. She also did not know that Lifen instructed Chung to tell the medical personnel that saving the egg for Yo was supposed to take precedence over saving her life in the car on the way to the hospital.

The nurse began to become further enraged as she realized that she would never see her sister's child. As all of the scenarios played out in her head, she saw General Chung's sister enter the hospital and did what the administrators instructed her to do.

Once the nurse informed her of the plan, General Chung's sister seemed delighted by the honor, knowing her family's well-being would be assured during and after the pregnancy.

With overwhelming emotions, the nurse began to prep for the procedure. The nurse prep station was located across the hall from an AIDS patient. The nurse began to think the unthinkable.

She looked at the syringes in the prep room and walked over to the patient's room. She pretended to look at his chart. "Hello, Mr. Choo. I am here to take a sample of your blood. We have a new program for AIDS patients, and your blood type may be eligible for the study."

The patient was extremely excited. Just hours before this nurse entered the room, a doctor had told him he had three months to live. The patient was too weak to speak any words, so he just lifted his arm so the nurse could take the blood.

The nurse quickly extracted the blood and placed a cap over the needle. She then ran to the operating room with the needle filled with infected blood in the pocket of her scrubs. She walked into the room and realized that everyone was ready to begin. She was the only person they were waiting for. General Chung's sister had not wanted to begin the procedure without the nurse who had informed her.

Standing at the threshold of the door with all eyes on her, the nurse looked down at General Chung's sister and noticed she was still awake and not fully sedated from the anesthesia. Once the general's sister saw the nurse at the door, she extended her arm out to the nurse, so that she could hold her hand during the surgery. The nurse rushed in and took her hand to comfort her.

While this was happening, a doctor entered the room of the AIDS patient and noticed his arm was bleeding. The doctor had been assigned to Mr. Choo for the past six months and was the only person to ever extract blood from him. The nurse was in such a rush to extract his blood that she didn't tie anything around his arm, so she missed his vein twice before she was able to correctly find one.

When the doctor noticed the blood on the patient's arm, he asked, "Mr. Choo, who did this to your arm?"

Mr. Choo was too weak to respond, so the doctor rushed out of the room to check the surveillance tapes. He was concerned that someone was tampering with Mr. Choo's medical regimen, which would jeopardize the research the doctor was doing.

Once he arrived to the security desk, he said to the guard, "Please check the tape for room nine forty-two on the fifth floor."

"Why?" the security guard asked.

"How dare you ask me why? Just do what the hell I told you to do," replied the doctor in a really heated manner. The threat of someone tampering with or stealing his research was huge, so his emotions were running high. He then looked at the security guard's badge to see his name. "Officer Luó, if you do not do what I tell you to do, I will not only have you fired, but I will beat the hell out of you, too."

Once the doctor began to make his hands into fists to further demonstrate his intent, the guard immediately responded. He put his password into his computer to access the camera footage. Both he and the doctor watched the footage of the nurse leaving Mr. Choo's room and putting something in her pocket. The doctor asked the officer to zoom in on the image to see who the woman was, and as the monitor inched closer and closer to her face, he recognized her. As soon as he was able to make out the image, he ran to her department to ask where she was.

"Nurse Dongmei was assigned to a classified operation, and I cannot tell you her location," responded the administrative assistant for the department.

"I have reason to believe this woman has infected blood from an AIDS patient and means to do harm to someone. You must tell me her location immediately," said the doctor frantically.

"What would make you think that Dongmei, who has an exceptional record, would do something that dishonorable? Not to mention she is my friend, and I know she wouldn't do something like that. I refuse to tell you anything. Besides, how do I know you are not looking to cause harm to someone and you are not just trying to gain access to the location, so you can complete your terrorist plot?" said the assistant.

The doctor's frustration became uncontainable. Looking very aggressive, he said, "If you don't believe me, keep the location to yourself, and just for my own peace of mind, you go check it out, but bring an officer with you."

Although she still believed her friend would not do anything wrong, the assistant was convinced by the look on the doctor's face that something was going on. So she complied and had an armed guard escort the doctor to the operating room as she tagged along. All three of them watched from the observation room, which had a bird's eye view of Dongmei holding Chung's sister's hand and stroking her hair to comfort her.

"It's been over ten minutes, and nothing has happened. This plot you came up with is in your mind! I am leaving," said the assistant. She turned around in an angry manner and stormed out of the room, slamming the door behind her.

"I will wait to see what happens now, so will you please stay behind with me?" the doctor asked the security guard. The guard nodded his head, and the two continued to observe the procedure.

From their position in the observation room, the doctor and guard were unable to see how badly Dongmei was sweating. She was torn by the anger of losing her sister and being a part of the operation that was responsible for killing her. When she mustered up enough confidence, she decided that she would inject General Chung's sister with the AIDS-infected blood. She convinced herself that she would never see the baby again and her family wouldn't be notified, so what would be the point of the general's sister living a great life?

But the process was taking too long to unfold, and the guard began to get restless.

"Sir, I must get back to my post. We have to go," he said.

"I would like to stay behind to watch the rest of the surgery," responded the doctor.

"I'm sorry sir, but you can't stay a long time because I have other rounds to make, and there are protocols in place that don't allow you to stay here alone," said the guard.

"Just give me a couple more minutes, and then we can leave," said the doctor.

The guard nodded his head in approval. Five more minutes passed, and even the doctor grew restless and began to question his own judgment of the nurse.

"I think I may have overreacted. We can go now," said the doctor.

The guard gestured for the doctor to leave the room first and opened the door for him. The doctor walked through the threshold of the door, and the guard went out after him. But just as the guard left the threshold, he turned around for one final glance of the nurse and saw her reaching into her pocket and pulling out the needle.

The guard immediately pulled the doctor back into the room and pointed towards the window in Dongmei's direction. Both men began banging on the window, but no one in the operating room could hear them.

Dongmei was clearly nervous, and she didn't want to be seen, so she took out the needle very slowly. Both the guard and the doctor rushed out of the observation room and ran for the entrance of the operating room, but the door was magnetically locked and could only be opened with a pin code.

"What is the code?" the doctor began screaming at the top of his lungs.

"I don't know the code. Only the administrators and medical personnel have it," responded the guard.

Once they realized they couldn't open the door, the doctor pulled on the handle with all of his might, but his attempts were unsuccessful. Both men were helpless and ran back to the observation room in hopes that Dongmei didn't stick General Chung's sister with the needle. Once the two men got back to the observation room, they began jumping up and down, trying to get the attention of the people in the operating room, so they could signal them to stop, but their attempts were unsuccessful. The medical personnel were concentrating on the task at hand and didn't even notice the two men trying to get their attention from outside the room.

The commotion the doctor and guard were making inside the room was so loud that people on the outside of the observation room were looking to see what was going on. The guard called for the assistant, but her desk was too far for her to hear him. Then he grabbed a chair and attempted to smash the observation window to break the glass. After two tries he realized his attempts were useless. Not even Dongmei heard the noise.

The two men witnessed Nurse Dongmei injecting General Chung's sister with the infected blood. The doctor was so hurt that he began to cry for General Chung's sister. The event seemed like it happened in slow motion. There was nothing they could do. The needle was empty.

The commotion must have caused someone to contact security because the guard with the pin code had come to the area to investigate the disturbance.

"Open the door!" screamed the guard.

The guard immediately recognized the other guard and opened the door as the two men immediately went to the entrance of the operating room and entered the room. The noise of the door opening suddenly scared everyone in the room. The guard rushed over to Dongmei and tackled her to the ground. His anger and lack of planning gave him too much momentum, and he rolled over after grabbing the nurse, so that she landed on top of him. With both her hands free, Nurse Dongmei reached in her pocket for the needle, and she stabbed the guard in the arm with it, exposing him to the virus as well.

The guard was so intent on apprehending the nurse; he completely ignored being stuck with the needle. He flipped her over onto her stomach and placed her in handcuffs.

"Murderers!" Dongmei screamed out. "Murderers! You bastards let my sister die for Emperor Yo, so make sure you let him know that he will never have children. North Korea! North Korea will save me!"

The guard immediately took the nurse away, and the doctors completed the process of fertilizing the egg.

Once the operation was over and everyone had been informed of what happened, one of the nurses said, "I wouldn't wish what happened to that woman on anyone. She is going to wake up and realize her brother is dead, and she was infected with the AIDS virus by the very nurse that she requested to be in the operation room to hold her hand."

Months passed before Yo fully recovered from his injury. The Chinese Secret Police interrogated Nurse Dongmei and learned that both she and her sister, Lifen, were spies for North Korea.

General Chung's sister fully contracted the AIDS virus and passed it to Yo's unborn son, who was born with HIV.

Once Yo was debriefed, he vowed to not only cure his son of this virus but to gain revenge on North Korea. Yo's real reason for wanting to destroy North Korea now wasn't for any oil; it was for what the country did to his personal life.

During the pregnancy, Yo enlisted the nation's best doctors to find a cure for the virus and authorized one billion dollars to fund their research. He also added an incentive of thirty million dollars to the doctor who found the cure in order to promote competition.

The cure was developed within six months of the pregnancy, and both General Chung's sister and Yo's son were cured. Yo decided to sell the cure to all nations in exchange for purchasing bonds in their governments.

The United States purchased the cure but not for the reasons Yo thought. Little did he know at that time, but America didn't want the cure to save lives. The government wanted to control the population. After studying the cure, American scientists developed a strain of AIDS that it would not work on. This strain was carefully dispersed back into the population and spread throughout Africa. The United States then sent the strain back to China, offering the carriers' immediate family members green cards and jobs in America to ensure the cure wouldn't be of any help to the Chinese in the future.

America outsmarted the Chinese by using the purchase of the bonds as a smoke screen, but the nation underestimated China's appetite and Yo's willingness to do whatever it took to win and gain revenge. Yo commissioned his nation's top economic advisors to calculate how many bonds it would take to control US currency.

The advisor informed Yo of the amount, but the yuan wasn't strong enough against the dollar to purchase the amount of bonds needed, so Yo began to open China's doors for economic expansion. Because of this, other nations did the same for China in exchange.

Yo understood that for China to compete with other nations, he would have to totally disregard the environment and manufacture products with cheap labor. So he deregulated all business and removed all laws pertaining to child labor.

Within twenty years, China began to export more goods than any other nation on the planet. Once Yo established China's dominance, he began to reduce Chinese imports and implement environmental and business regulations and blame the reduction on capitalism threatening China's communist values. By that time, other nations were so dependent on Chinese manufacturers that they could not do the same with China, and any nation that attempted to do so was threatened with China flooding the market with the bonds they purchased over the last thirty years.

But the downside to this was that the Chinese people still longed to leave China, and that devastated Yo.

Yo's reflection was interrupted by his son bringing him his drink. He often questioned his fatherhood status and wondered how his son was affected by not knowing of his past except for the few stories Yo told him. Yo regretted his son not being nurtured by a woman who was his real mother, but how could he tell his son that his mother was killed by a North Korean who was a part of his inner and most trusted circle, and he didn't even know about it?

Yo was then distracted by the sight of Chancellor Merchant on the television giving a live interview with news reporter John Stevenson.

Roderik Von Merchant

"So, Chancellor Merchant, are you enjoying your stay in the United States?" asked Stevenson.

"I am. This is a beautiful country. I am proud to be in a place where Germany's economic and political partnerships are prosperous. It also warms me that my personal friendship with this country's leader is strong. I can honestly say that President Johnson has been a great friend, and his accommodations are appreciated," replied Merchant.

Stevenson was a seasoned interviewer, and he always knew that if a person used certain phrases or words such as "honestly," "to tell you the truth," and "between me and you," the person was more than likely lying. The idea is the person saying these phrases is subconsciously preparing the listener for a lie by making him or her comfortable and earning his or her trust with such phrases. Little did Stevenson know that Merchant's answer was strictly political, because his mind was still in the meeting room, and he was thinking about what Garçon had whispered to him. As Stevenson continued to ask his questions, Merchant was in a daze as if he were suspended in air. He was only able to answer a few of Stevenson's questions without asking him to repeat them, and all his questions received generic replies with no emotion.

The interview was so dry that while on air, Stevenson asked him, "Chancellor Merchant, are you OK?"

Anyone watching was able to see that Merchant's thoughts were clearly on something else. Once Stevenson asked him that question, the respect he had for Merchant's position went out the window. Now it was time for Stevenson to save the interview and show Merchant that when people get in his chair on his show, their minds should be totally devoted to paying attention to his questions.

Merchant was a seasoned interviewee, but today his patience was short, and in his mind it was clear the interview was already headed downhill. The longer the interview went on, the more annoyed Merchant became.

Stevenson has been through interviews like this many times before, and as a reporter he knew one way to spice up a dry interview is through more questions. He knew if he asked more questions, Merchant would become increasingly frustrated because he didn't want to be there. And the more frustrated Merchant got, the more likely it was that he would say something out of the ordinary or storm off. Stevenson's ego never let him take the blame for a poor interview, but if the subject stormed off, the reporter would gain credibility from the audience regardless of how talented the interviewer was during the interview.

"I understand you and President Johnson have maintained a friendship for quite some time," Stevenson began.

"We have," said Merchant in an unemotional manner.

"So, what do you think he learned about you today in your meeting with him that he didn't know before?" asked Stevenson.

Although Garçon had said Merchant's secret in his ear and only he heard it, Merchant's paranoia didn't let him feel at ease. It didn't matter that Garçon whispered his secret just to him because in Merchant's mind it was nothing short of him saying it on a loud speaker at a soccer game. Merchant wanted to get away to think, and finishing this interview was the last thing on his mind, so he did what any man in power would do: he used his responsibilities as an excuse as to why he had to leave.

"I am sorry, Mr. Stevenson, but we will have to wrap up this interview. I am here in the States for such a short period of time, and I am mourning the death of a truly special person. My mind just isn't where it needs to be, so feel free to ask your last question, and to make it up to you, I will provide you with additional time for more questions once I am back in Germany," stated Merchant as he used the death of Vice President Perez as an excuse to conclude the interview.

Merchant's response was elegant. He found a way to give Stevenson an out, and he was able to maintain his calm demeanor on national television. The voices in Stevenson's earpiece were telling him to discuss Merchant's conservative views on gays in his country. The control room wanted to get his insight about gay marriage being legalized on a national level when the Supreme Court voted in favor of the measure by a wide range of six to three in America. With Obama appointing four judges during his presidency, the only conservative judges left were appointed by the Rubio administration. Stevenson, an

Emmy award winning journalist, knew if he took that order, Merchant would not grant him another interview.

"Chancellor Merchant, I am going to allow you to continue with your affairs regarding your grief and conclude this interview so that you can mourn accordingly. I do hope you find a way to enjoy the rest of your trip and try not to think about trying to save the world while you are here," said Stevenson.

The camera clicked off, but the control room was furious, screaming at Stevenson through his earpiece.

Stevenson responded calmly, "Why alienate the man further by pressing the issue? His mind was clearly on something else, and asking him that would have prevented us from getting another interview in the future."

The voices in his ear went silent, but Stevenson could still hear frustrated breaths from the control room.

"Thank you, Stevenson," said Merchant, who was notoriously paranoid. Reflecting on Stevenson's last comment about saving the world, he began to wonder if Stevenson knew more about the meeting than Merchant thought he did. Little did he know that the control room was trying to get Stevenson to speak on the rights of gays in his country. Had he, he would have immediately become even more paranoid.

As he began to take off the audio equipment so that he could leave the studio, his hatred toward Garçon began to grow more than ever.

With Garçon never being married and fighting for the equality of gay people in France, Merchant was able to rest assured that his secret was safe because Garçon was the perfect leader to keep the focus off of Merchant's secret lifestyle.

As he walked down the hall to his dressing room with his security detail, Merchant's paranoia made him begin to look at each of them as potential leaks. First, there was Felix Adenauer, his guard for five years. Felix was a man of true honor and integrity, and he was someone Merchant would never second-guess under any circumstances, except for this one.

Felix never left his side, and the two even talked about Felix's training in the German Special Forces and his evaluations to join Merchant's personal guard. Military personnel would study every physical and mental inch of the soldiers attempting to join. Physiological specialists were trained to develop testing that would allow the German military to know these soldiers better than they knew themselves. Any soldier could train for the team, and 99 percent of the applicants passed the physical portion of the testing, but only a select few were able to pass the psychological testing. Only those who could do that were allowed to join.

Based on the tests, military leadership would assess the limits of the soldiers and force them to commit an act that would require the soldiers to push how far they were willing to go to be members of the squad. The rationale behind this was that to honestly protect someone else, soldiers' personal hang-ups must be totally disregarded. There must not be any thought or hesitation as to what the soldiers would or wouldn't do to protect the chancellor or any other leaders they were assigned to, and there was only one way to find that out. Publicly, Merchant denounced Adolf Hitler, but behind closed doors he secretly embraced the old dictator's training methods.

Based on his profile, Felix was a known ladies' man and borderline sex addict.

During Felix's training, German army personnel sprayed perfume on the ground where he would lay down in the sniper position for target practice, and then they studied his reaction once he caught a whiff of the scent. Each time he smelled the perfume, he looked around to see if a woman was present. His gestures were always subtle, so to regular civilians the actions would be totally undetectable, but to individuals studying him, they meant everything. On days the perfume was sprayed, he scored higher than on days he was shooting with no scent in the bunker.

According to all psychological tests, Felix performed higher on the days the perfume was sprayed because he instinctively thought he needed to impress a woman if she was completing the grading or doing the evaluation. Once he completed his assessments, he was asked if he noticed the smell in the bunkers.

"Yes," Felix replied.

The assessor then asked, "How did you feel about that?"

Felix replied, "I thought one of the women associated with your department prepared the bunker prior to me getting there, and I wanted to impress her with my skill even though I had no idea what she looked like. Every time I'd lay in that bunker, I imagined Elga Schwartz. She had the nicest hair and smelled just like that fragrance. I lost her to one of my school buddies on the rugby team. I would just imagine hitting that target and her being so overwhelmed by my performance that she would run across that field and jump into my arms. I was disappointed each day that I would see your ugly mugs instead of hers. All the other days I didn't smell the fragrance just ran together. But the days when I smelled that perfume, it took me to a place that reminded me of better days."

His answers were great, and there was nothing that could be taken away from him that would really matter except one thing. Felix was a heterosexual man by every measure, so asking him to be with another man was the only way to test his commitment to the program. When the proposition was suggested to Felix, he was genuinely offended, but his reply was flawless. The day the offer and initiation was presented, the room was filled with men and one woman.

Once Felix disregarded his personal feelings, he said, "If you will have me do this, how long do I have to complete the act?"

"You will have five hours," said Edwards, one of the evaluators.

"Five hours? That's it?" replied Felix.

"Well, five hours is more than enough time. In the field, you will be required to make decisions in less time than that. We believe that amount of time is generous," Edwards responded.

"That makes sense. Are there any more rules I should be aware of?" asked Felix.

"No, that is all. A sexual act with a man."

Felix surveyed the room and realized Edwards was too far away from him to grab, but he noticed one of the other psychologists sitting to the right of him. Felix made a fist with his right hand and smashed the left hand of the psychologist, which was palm down on the table. He then grabbed the psychologist by the neck and smashed his head on the table, knocking the man clean out.

The room was totally horrified by Felix's unexpected turn. They began to huddle together, as if being in a group would somehow protect them as they hoped not to be next. The group then collectively migrated toward the corner of the room. With the entire room of psychologists horrified and in the corner, the only way for any of them to get out, would be to pass Felix, and no one was willing to take that chance out of fear he or she would be harmed.

Felix looked at them and screamed, "Look at you, all huddled together with no one willing to pass me to get out of the room, and no one willing to help your fellow colleague here. At the end of the day, it's all about self-preservation for each of you, isn't it? Before I begin, I would like to state this for the record. I want you to change the procedure and make the interviewees sit as far away from the exit as possible, because the way you each positioned me, all of you can die instead of one or two sacrificial lambs. Second, I am very interested in staying in this program; I am just doing this to prove a point, so you idiots can be satisfied."

The room was secure and did not have any communication devices in it for the doctors to call security, so unless one of them was willing to make a run for the door, they were at Felix's mercy. Felix began to unbuckle the pants of the doctor he had just knocked out. The anger in Felix's face was real, and the emotion from the doctors was so thick that all of them were frozen in fear. Felix began to force the doctor's pants down so hard he was ripping the side of the waist.

"Look at how scared you look!" Felix said. "Oh, it's OK to test my commitment to the program, but why should my commitment be the only one tested?" He then started to unbuckle his own pants.

"I wish this was you, Edwards, but now that I think of it, you would be knocked out, and your facial expression is good enough."

"Don't do this!" said Edwards.

"I don't want to do this. But this is what you made me do. I asked if there were any rules, and you clearly stated that completing the task was the only rule," Felix said.

With Felix's pants all the way down, he began to enter the doctor while looking directly at Edwards. Everyone in the room could see he was holding back tears and was not enjoying what he was doing at all. After five pumps, the doctor, still knocked out and laying with half his body on the table and the other half sliding off without Felix there to support him, slid all the way off the table, his head hitting the floor.

The sound startled all of the doctors, and Felix said to them, "I didn't want to do that, but if my commitment to this program requires me to do anything regardless of if I do or do not agree with it, then I will do it!"

The doctors never expected such a response from a recruit. In their subsequent reports they noted that Felix's abilities to survey his surrounding and establish solutions were extraordinary.

The doctor that Felix penetrated resigned that day after being revived and was never again heard from by his colleagues. When asked why was he leaving, he stated, "How can I come to work and look at those people in the eye, the same people who stood by and watched that happen to me without attempting to help me? How can those men and that woman evaluate personnel on completing something that they were not willing to do themselves? I am not mad at what happened; I thought his response was genius because it was something I didn't account for. To think I was eager to see how he would have handled that prerequisite if he actually left the room. But we were OK with it happening to someone else as long as it was not one of us, and I no longer believe in that."

As Merchant reflected on Felix's story, he looked over his left shoulder for the guard. He saw Felix standing in his combat-ready position. Felix's eyes met with Merchant's, and Felix discreetly gave him a nod to indicate his assurance that the environment was under control.

Standing next to Felix was William. A graduate at the top of his class in the German Military Academy, William could have worked in the private sector at any world renowned company but decided to pursue a career in the military. He specifically wanted to protect the chancellor of Germany because he was so determined and ambitious that his only motivation was to be next to one of the most powerful figures in the world. Merchant looked at William and reflected on the fact that William almost did not get into the program because he had a twin brother who looked exactly like him.

The agency typically stayed away from applicants with twins because it left open the possibility that one of the twins could potentially impersonate the other. During World War II, one of Hitler's most trusted generals was a twin. His name was Erik Bohm, and French spies attempted to kidnap him and switch him with his twin brother, Garin, to gain valuable intelligence during the war. Garin grew up in Germany but was sent to France away from his family to integrate into French culture. At the end of World War I, Germany sent numerous children into France to act as spies for the German government. These children were vetted and sent back to Germany frequently, so they would not lose their German roots but the government did want them to develop French accents in order to be more effective spies, which was why they were sent so young. The German government had a fascination with twins because they believed they could be controlled more easily by making threats to the other twin.

The German program leaders had planned to promote both Erik and Garin at the same time, but when Garin fell behind Erik, jealousy and resentment drove them apart. Garin felt that Erik was able to advance due to his ability to stay in Germany. He felt that being stationed in France had hindered his brotherly bond with Erik, and soon the bond turned to bitter rivalry. Communication during that era was difficult, and Erik did not go to France because he did not want to blow Garin's cover. Erik was unable to follow Garin's progress or provide reassurance that his suspicions of betrayal were unwarranted.

As time passed and World War II became inevitable, Garin became even more jealous of his brother and disgusted with the German government. Feeling as though he was abandoned and not brought back to Germany as a war strategist, especially after Germany beat France in such a short period of time, Garin thought there was no way he would continue to be a spy for the German government. His anger drove him to become a member of the French Anti-Nazi party, and when France fell to Germany and didn't bring him home, he immediately told the French who he was.

Erik had not seen his brother for such a long time that Garin didn't know Erik had told Hitler he had a twin. Hitler immediately branded an "SS" on the bottom of Erik's foot. The French began to prep Garin for taking Erik's place and executed the plan to kidnap Erik flawlessly in the bathroom stall of a hotel. The next day Garin reported to Hitler as Erik did every day but was not prepared for what would happen next. Garin didn't know that Hitler's morning ritual was to have Erik take off his shoes to reveal the branding on the bottom of his foot. French intelligence were unaware of this because the mark was located on the bottom of Erik's foot, and their spies had never seen Erik's bare feet, even during sex, as they had sent in French women to monitor him.

When Erik revealed to Hitler that he was a twin, Hitler thought the possibility of one of Germany's enemies attempting this tactic was imminent. As Erik's relationship and position with Hitler grew, Hitler felt that it was necessary to protect himself. Once Garin's foot exposed the plot, Garin was killed, and all identical twins after that were expelled from all high-level positions in German government.

William's physical and mental performance results were so exceptional that the agency allowed to him to join the program under the one condition, a condition Hitler later applied to the bylaws: if the twin successfully terminated any and all siblings having a similar physical appearance to the selected member, then that individual would be allowed to join the agency.

William never had an issue with killing anyone but what had made this task easier was that his brother was addicted to drugs. As his evaluators gave him the requirements for him to fulfill in order to be in the program, William sat in his chair, stone-faced, only nodding his head in agreement.

He opened his mouth only to say, "I haven't seen Ahren in over five years. I will do what it takes to join, but the last time I heard about him, he was on drugs and was no longer able to stay with our parents because he sold their jewelry to buy drugs."

The evaluators in the room anticipated his response and waited until William finished talking to hand him a file. William didn't attempt to open it until one of the evaluators instructed him to do so.

"Your brother's location is within that envelope. All the information you need can be found in the envelope as well. Once you land, you will have five hours to complete your task," said the lead evaluator.

"Before I land? Land where?" asked William.

As William looked for answers, all the men and women in the room stood up to leave the room and ignored his question. He asked it again, but with no success; he still wasn't given an answer by anyone in the room. Realizing his questions were falling on deaf ears, he decided to open the envelope. He then realized that for the first time in five years, he would be able to see his brother, but under terrible circumstances. He saw a plane ticket for New York, New York, and the paperwork indicated that Ahren had been living there for four years.

For the first time in his life, William felt uncertain about his next move. Killing his twin brother five years ago would have been easy, but any agency that Merchant was a part of would never make anything easy. William had to prepare himself for anything. As he continued to look through the packet, he realized that his flight to New York was leaving in three hours.

Of course, there wasn't any passport information in the packet, so if he were to get caught, the German government would deny he ever existed. This was going to have to be done cleanly and without a trace. But how could he do it without getting caught?

William asked himself, "Is all this worth being in the agency?"

Once he confirmed that his answer was yes, he started to wonder what the other soldiers had to do. If William didn't have a twin brother, what other task would the evaluators have come up with to make him prove himself? The reflections began to overwhelm him to the point that he didn't realize he had left his home and was in a taxi at the airport. The only thing that was able to break his concentration was the cab driver asking him for money to pay the fare, money that the agency didn't provide him with.

Did they only supply him with a plane ticket, time frame, and address for a reason? He began to think this could be a set up until a security officer stopped him from walking to his gate.

"Please follow me, sir," said the officer.

Despite maintaining an emotionless face, William felt his heart sink in his stomach. He only imagined the worst happening to him as the officer escorted him to a private room. The people in the airport were looking at William being escorted away as if there were something wrong. Once William walked through the door, he saw three of the evaluators who gave him the assignment. They were eager to talk to him.

"William, congratulations! You have passed your first test," the first evaluator said.

"What test is that?" William asked.

"You displayed total disregard for your life and freedom by knowingly using your own money and identification to initiate this mission. The fact that you used your personal passport indicates to the agency that it doesn't have to worry about any other identities or your assuming the identity of your brother. A man with your personality traits usually has something to hide, and we are glad you proved us incorrect. If you are going to protect the chancellor, that type of selflessness and stability is required."

"Just curious," the second evaluator said. "With New York having some of the strictest gun and weapons laws in America, how are you going to kill him? Especially since your file has not shown any known friends or family in that area other than your brother."

"Peanut poison. My brother has a deadly reaction to peanuts, so peanuts are a very cheap way to get this thing done. Plus, I have a feeling that he has gotten his life in order, which I am sure you already knew and I was a going to find out once I got to America. Before I left, I checked his Facebook page on my phone and his page is public. I wanted to see if he had any kids or a spouse, and I saw that he does, so I checked to make sure he didn't have any girls—"

That statement was intriguing to one of the evaluators, so she cut William off and asked, "Why does the gender of the children matter?"

"If he had a girl, I would say fuck this program, because little girls who grow up without a father are emotional wrecks. How selfish would I be not only to kill my brother but also to leave his wife alone to raise his girls and then those young ladies grow up emotionally unstable? Girls who grow up without a father can be either sexually promiscuous or emotionally withdrawn and it would be because of my selfishness and ambition."

"What about the boys?" asked another evaluator.

"The boys will be fine. They will have been born of fine genes and with an unquenchable desire to protect their mother by trying to take up the slack left by their dad not being there. I will go back to check on them, and with me looking like their dad, I will be able to provide them with the guidance they need to be productive citizens in life," responded William.

"Will you please wait outside?" the first evaluator asked.

William did as instructed, but he wasn't sure if he should remind them of their deadline and that his flight was set to leave in forty minutes. Within ten minutes, William was asked to come back into the room.

The first evaluator asked, "Are you willing to do what it takes to be a part of the agency?"

William looked at evaluators with a puzzled face and said, "I was on the way to kill my own brother. I thought we were clear on my answer."

One of the men repeated the question. "Are you willing to do whatever it takes to be a part of the agency?"

William realized they wanted a straight answer and that giving a witty answer was not going to be tolerated.

"Yes, I am."

"There is no turning back now," the first evaluator said as he pulled out a gun and shot a dart at William. William had anticipated something was going to happen and swiftly moved to his left, catching the dart with his bare hand. He looked at it with a puzzled expression.

"Why?"

The whole room paused. The evaluators had never seen something like that before, and even William had surprised himself by being able to catch the dart. Once the pause was over, the evaluator released two more shots aimed at William's arm and leg. William was able to dodge one dart, but the other dart hit him in the leg, and he immediately began to feel drowsy.

Before he fully fell asleep, he heard a voice say, "William, you are quite an amazing solider. I understand you don't trust us, but I need you to trust the agency. We want you to protect the chancellor of our great country, but how do we ensure you are capable of doing that if we don't test you? I am saying to trust the agency because your trust will be vital for this country, your unit, and the chancellor. Your body will undergo some extreme changes shortly. We shot you with the dart to let you know we are no longer requiring you to kill your brother. Make no mistake. Only under special circumstances is completing your final task waived, but there are a few twists that have to be ironed out immediately."

The lead evaluator pulled out another weapon that he pointed at William and laid it on the table. Once he laid the gun on the table, he gave a hand gesture to the others in the room to help him turn William on his stomach. A doctor stood over William on the table and stuck the barrel of the gun in William's neck, injecting him with serum filled with microscopic tracking devices. Half of the devices would remain in William's blood as long as he stayed with the agency, and the other half attached to his spinal cord. Once the injection was complete, the evaluators turned William around and held him up.

William was a military man, so he followed orders without question, and although he was fuming on the inside, he completely understood the reason this was being done.

"I am happy that I didn't have to kill my brother," William said as he started to regain motion in his body.

"We are as well, but please know we have injected your brother with a similar device to ensure we are able to keep tabs on him as well," replied the evaluator.

"How did you inject him?" William asked.

"It's dinner time in New York City right now. Once we saw you at the airport, we simply notified our contact in the area, and he placed the tracking devices in his drink while he was at dinner with his family. I was told that the poor guy nearly choked to death at dinner," the evaluator replied with a chuckle.

William looked at the evaluator with disdain and said, "Why didn't you give me that option?"

"Your job in the agency is not about choice; it is about sacrifice. If someone tries to kill our chancellor, you will be required to make a choice to give your life for someone else or save your own. Once you applied to be in this agency, your choices are no longer yours, and this is one of those instances where we are showing you that. If you want out, go. If not, report for duty in two weeks at this address." The evaluator placed an envelope on the table and then left the room.

Merchant realized that William was a dedicated guard who would never let anyone know his secret, but due to his current state of paranoia, that didn't prevent him from having a bit of suspicion towards William especially with him harboring potential for bitterness toward the agency for attempting to make him kill his brother. Merchant was not clear if William's resentment had passed.

He then glanced over to George and began to evaluate if he was the one who had told. Merchant always admired George because he was structured and thorough. He was the kind of man who thought of all the ins and outs of his life and left nothing to chance.

As Merchant reflected on George's service, he couldn't imagine a man as dedicated as him ever telling anyone anything, especially a secret that would turn his country upside down. Merchant knew George never agreed with the chancellor's secret life, but his honor to his country, his extreme patriotism, would make him swallow his pride enough to think only about the greater good of the nation.

George grew up in the slums of Germany. According to his files, he never knew his father, and his mother was unable to have any more children because of complications with her pregnancy with George.

This was a secret that his mother never expressed to him. George's grandfather was a war veteran with a heavy drinking problem. The problem was so bad that he nearly killed George's mother and grandmother while driving them home from the hospital the day after George was born. As time passed, George's grandmother and mother left his grandfather and moved to Berlin, but no matter how many times they moved or tried to avoid him, his grandfather would find a way to locate them. Since he was a high-ranking German army officer, his grandfather was able to use his military connections to always keep tabs on both George's mother and grandmother.

One day when George was a teenage boy, his grandfather surprised him while he was on his way to school and injected George with a serum that knocked him out immediately. When George awoke, he found that his grandfather had him tied in a chair in an abandoned basement. He looked around in terror. At that time, George had no clue who this man was, and he immediately began to cry uncontrollably.

"Do you know who I am?" asked his grandfather.

"No. I only know I want to go home," George replied, sobbing uncontrollably.

"I am your grandfather," he smugly replied.

"If you are my grandfather, then why do you have me tied in this chair?" asked George.

"Because I am going to make sure your mother and grandmother know I found them," his grandfather replied.

George noticed that his grandfather had a piece of iron in a fire burning red hot.

"I am going to burn my initials on your arm, so you and those bitches will never forget me," he said as he took a gulp of the liquor in his flask.

George saw his grandfather turn around to get the piece of iron, and he began to struggle in the chair, causing one of the legs to break and loosening all the ropes that held him down. His grandfather turned back around to face him, and the two began to struggle over the heated iron rod. George was tall for his age and was able to match strength for strength with his grandfather, who was still in great shape for his age.

As his grandfather began to tire out, George began to push him back towards a sharp metal beam that was protruding from the wall. George realized he had the upper hand and began to drive his grandfather closer and closer toward the metal with tremendous force.

Gaining more and more anger and confidence with each step, he was able to push his grandfather back until he eventually pushed the older man into the piece of iron protruding from the wall. His grandfather was too exhausted from the struggle to pull himself from the metal and immediately began to fade in and out of consciousness.

George grabbed his backpack and ran out of the building. By recognizing the landmarks in the area, he was able to run home.

George never told anyone of what he did, and the police never pursued his grandfather's killer because they were able to link his DNA to multiple murders in southern Germany. By reviewing the crime scene, the police deduced that the victim had escaped and the old man lost the battle. George's shoe size was big enough to mistake for a grown man's, and George's grandfather had prepared the scene in a way that no physical evidence could be linked back to George. George did not know this was the case, so he lived as if he was on the run and the police would find him at any moment. He was constantly covering his tracks with everything he did.

As he grew up, George resented the fact that his grandfather made his mother feel like she was always on the run and had caused George to feel that way as well now. As time went on, George could no longer control his paranoia, and it began to get the better of him. The last straw was when the German Parliament passed a law requiring all German police officers to carry fingerprint scanners as well as granting them the right to arrest any citizens that they deemed to be threatening based on body language and the tone of their voice. This governmental power made George so nervous about killing his grandfather that he decided to join the police department, so he could put an end to his torment.

He had been fingerprinted many times throughout his life, but he was never as nervous about it as he was the day he joined the police. The whole night he didn't sleep a wink, wondering if the police would knock on his door to arrest him or if they would just wait for him to show up at the training facilities and arrest him there. As morning came, George contemplated not showing up, but he was sick of living in fear. He needed the job to make sure he could access the mainframe computers to ensure he didn't have to live in fear any more. As he entered the academy, he realized that day was just like any other day. No one was there to arrest him, and his superior officers were all eager to see him to congratulate him for passing all the tests to join the force.

George's scores were high enough that he was awarded the duty of leading a small antiterrorism unit within the department. The position was a total shock to him. Being the group leader, George was able to gain access to all the documents about his grandfather's death without any questions or suspicions arising about him accessing the files. George knew that even if someone had questioned him, he would just state that he wanted to see the files to gain some insight to the case and to capture the killer, since the case had inspired him to become a police officer in the first place.

As George accessed the files, he realized that the police had nothing. Because he was big for his age, the police had assumed based on the shoe prints left at the scene and the strength it took to break loose from the chair that the killer was a full-grown man. Once the police found that his grandfather's DNA matched the DNA found at other murder sites, they never suspected that the person who escaped was a young boy because that didn't fit the characteristics of the other victims.

Once George realized this, it was like the weight of the world was lifted off of his shoulders. He quickly rose through the police ranks, catching the eye of the agency. Once they began testing him, he easily met all of their requirements and soon only his last test remained.

The evaluators realized how structured George was, and one of his major attributes was how strategic he was, so his final test was being dropped off in a third-world country with no money or identification and no way to call anyone to assist him. He was required to get back to Germany by any means necessary within seventy-two hours. George didn't think the evaluators were aware of his past, so they wouldn't know that George had been preparing for this moment his whole life, living on the edge and practicing escaping Germany so he wouldn't go to jail. That mind-set and the skills he learned while training for law enforcement only added on to his ability to be prepared for anything.

George was dropped off in the city of Safi located in the country of Morocco. Safi was a port city on the Atlantic Ocean, so George was able to travel from Safi to Spain by hitching a ride on a millionaire singer's yacht. George posed as the replacement staff for a man that he had drugged so he could take his place on the vessel. George's presence on the boat was never questioned because the amount of drugs on the boat was endless. The singer himself had never experienced such a situation, so he was just happy to be a part of the action and didn't ask any questions for fear of causing a disturbance that would end all the fun he and his friends were having.

George had worked as a waiter and chef in a busy downtown Berlin restaurant growing up, so he was able to utilize his service skills while on the boat and even assisted the chef with a couple of meals.

Although the trip lasted under three days, George was anxious about making sure he met the seventy-two-hour deadline. Once the boat arrived in the Spanish port, George began to exit the

175

ship when he noticed two evaluators from the agency waiting for him.

He was actually happy to see them, but no one would ever know that based on his blank facial expression. He met both men and shook their hands.

While they began to walk toward the car, one evaluator asked, "Was catching that boat destiny, or was it luck?"

"Sometimes I like to think I control my own destiny, but I feel that some things don't need explanation. It's best if you just sit back and enjoy the ride. But I thought you wanted me to get back to Germany. Why are you here in Spain?" replied George.

The evaluator replied, "We are aware of your issues with your grandfather. Getting back to Germany from Spain was never an issue for you. The captain of the ship is actually a German operative we use to keep tabs on celebrities throughout the world, so once he saw you on the ship, he contacted us to make sure we were aware of the situation and your location. We are everywhere, George."

The evaluator was looking for some type of emotion from George, but he wasn't going to get that.

Once the car stopped and the door opened, George saw Merchant waiting outside for him. He immediately knew what his assignment would be. He got out of the car, and the two shook hands.

Merchant pulled George in close and whispered in his ear, "You made a name for yourself. To go from killing a man as a child to protecting the chancellor of Germany is a feat in itself."

George pulled back while still maintaining the handshake. Before he was totally deflated, Merchant shook his hand tighter and nodded to assure George that his secret was safe with him.

That day George's loyalty to Merchant was sealed, and as Merchant ended his reflection on George, he knew it wasn't George who told. With both men understanding the importance of discretion and the potential of losing everything, Merchant didn't think twice about if George had leaked his secret.

Merchant then turned his attention to Spencer. Spencer was the doctor of the team, but he was also trained in combat. Merchant was always paranoid and felt that someone would try to assassinate him at some point, so he wanted to have a trained medical doctor with him at all times who would be able to treat traumatic wounds with limited supplies and equipment, someone who could service a wound long enough to get him to a hospital in order for proper surgery to be completed. Merchant felt that this position was of utmost importance. The other posts in the security detail required 90 percent brawn and 10 percent coordination or intellect. The position of the chancellor's protective surgeon required a combination of brains, calm, and resourcefulness to effectively do the job, especially during an assassination attempt.

Merchant felt so strongly about this that when he was given a list of qualified medical doctors who had passed both the medical training and the sharp shooting tests, he instructed the agency to put them through another form of training instead of making them do an extraordinary act.

Merchant would send chimpanzees into a battlefield to be shot in combat situations. Because the chimps' anatomy was the closest to humans' of any animals, the doctors were required to perform surgery on the chimps with gunfire surrounding them.

Merchant instructed the agency to dismiss any doctor who questioned whether the chimps were disease-free because that was an indication they did not fully trust the agency to take care of them and provide them with a safe training environment. If their sole purpose was to protect and save the life of the chancellor, the doctors wouldn't think twice about performing any procedures in real time regardless of Merchant's medical status.

To Merchant's surprise, only five out of thirty-seven men who passed were dismissed for asking if the chimps were safe. When Merchant heard that amount, he replied in a steely tone, "At least we saved five chimps."

The snipers, who were also training for the agency, were instructed to hit the chimps above an artery in either the thigh or in the neck on either side. The bullets were coated with a strong sedative, so the animals would remain calm while the

179

doctors attempted to save their lives and so they would not feel any pain in the process. The doctors would be responsible for patching the wounds amid gunfire all around them. Whoever was able to save their chimps long enough to get them to the hospital would be able to move to the next round.

Out of the thirty-two remaining doctors, only three were able to save their chimps while under fire. Ten doctors actually experienced panic attacks while trying to save the chimps in the field.

Merchant was an avid boxing and mixed martial arts fan, so the three remaining doctors were instructed to be the cut men for fighters fighting on a given night. If the fighters were cut during their fights, the doctors were instructed to stop the bleeding within one minute with any material deemed legal by the German Fight Commission.

Merchant felt this would be a clean-cut example of a doctor working under a high-pressure, timed situation without actually putting a human in harm's way. Two out of the remaining three doctors were able to stop the bleeding from cuts their fighters sustained during their fights, so Merchant instructed the agency to keep both the doctors on staff to alternate their duties.

Although both doctors were protecting Merchant, Spencer slowly started becoming Merchant's main doctor and was granted all of the assignments that exposed Merchant's other life. The other doctor, Friedrich, only received low-level assignments during which Merchant wouldn't dare engage in his secret behavior.

Merchant liked Spencer because he had a swagger to him that Merchant admired. The fact that Spencer was also a good-looking doctor who was able to defend himself with deadly force when necessary made Merchant admire him even more. Friedrich was a great doctor, but no one you would want to hang out and have a drink with. Merchant also believed in gene superiority, and in his eyes, Spencer was the perfect person a woman could have sex with to ensure proper offspring. Although he was not the type of man Merchant was attracted to, Merchant enjoyed the camaraderie he and Spencer shared. Spencer could care less about Merchant's secret life, and Merchant knew that, which is why he ruled out Spencer as the suspect who told Garçon. But who could it be? Who would tell Garçon about Fehrenbach?

As ruthless as Merchant was, he would not have any problem killing one of his trusted guards, and if one of them did tell someone, that is what would happen. But he was positive the men he had guarding him would never betray him to Garçon and expose him to world.

Merchant's saving grace was that the world was in a dire situation. Garçon wouldn't expose his secret because bringing another leader into these discussions would be a tremendous variable that could throw off the plan already set in motion but Merchant still wanted to know.

As his mind became consumed with indecision, his phone began to ring. He glanced at the caller's number and then picked up.

"Hello, my dear. How have you been?" said Merchant.

Merchant's wife responded, "Fantastic as usual. Will I be seeing you tonight?"

"Not tonight, honey. I have to run. I have urgent business to take care of," replied Merchant.

He hung up and then immediately went to Google on his smartphone. Once the website popped up, he set up a news alert for Anton Garçon, President of France. Merchant could easily have his intelligence agency find out everything and send him the information, but for some reason setting up the Google alert made him feel as if he was in control. As soon as he completed the notification settings, a Google alert came on of Garçon sitting in his car with a puzzled look on his face with the caption, "What is the most eligible bachelor in the world thinking?"

Merchant's blood began to boil because he was no closer to knowing how Garçon had found out his secret.

Anton Garçon

As Garçon sat back in his car and reflected on his fight with Merchant while people were taking pictures of him until his driver pulled off, he came to the conclusion that he did not regret saying what he said to Merchant. The information he had received about the world ending did not bother him. The only thing on his mind was that he had no one to be with him during this time. What if he were not the president of France? What then? Would he still be alone? As he thought about Vice President Perez, he envisioned his own funeral with no wife or children there to mourn him.

Garçon was never one to focus on the options he had, but he always reflected on the options he didn't have. His whole life was geared toward trying to impress Christina. He was constantly scheming to try to get her to leave her husband for him. He was constantly trying to stay in shape so she would love his body. He was constantly trying to be loved by her. His pursuit of finding a way for her to forever regret her decision never to leave her husband to be with Garçon was exhausting.

Even after today's meeting, his thoughts were not about her kids or her life; he could care less about that. His thoughts were solely on how he could manufacture a way to get rid of her husband, so she wouldn't feel the guilt of leaving him.

Garçon admired Christina because she always kept him on his toes. When she told him she loved him, Garçon never knew if she meant it or if she was giving him lip service because he was powerful and needed to hear her words for affirmation. To him, it did not matter either way because all he cared about was being with her, whether it was for an hour or a day.

He still reflected on the first time they met while he was a soccer player at college. Even then, she was with someone. Coming off a match against a rival, he went to a bar. There she stood in the corner of the room having a drink alone. He realized that she wanted to be alone because every man that came up to her was turned away, but he looked at her as a challenge. Her rejection of others had awakened every sexual impulse in him. Feeling high off of scoring the winning goal, he walked over to her, but before he could sneak up to her, she spotted him approaching because she observed her surroundings like a tigress looking for a safe place for her cubs.

185

Armed with his confidence and the colors of his soccer team's uniform, he strutted over in a way that reminded her of a male peacock showing off his feathers to her. But his aura had her confused about her plan for that evening. She wanted to be alone, but she was intrigued by his swagger. As he got closer, she decided to give him a smile instead of preparing to push him away. Before she knew it, her smile turned into eye contact, and that was all Garçon needed. Once their eyes met, she dipped the left side of her chin into the left side of her shoulder, which made her hair fall into her face, covering her eyes and smile, but her disguise was too late because Garçon was the master of observation. She was too late to hide anything from him if that was her intention.

Garçon always assessed people for weaknesses, so he could gain an advantage over them. As Christina continued to smile at him, he walked faster and sat in the booth with her. She kept her chin dipped in her shoulder for what seemed like an eternity, but that did not deter Garçon. He stayed in the booth with her and waved over the waitress to order some drinks for both of them.

Christina's hair didn't allow her to see Garçon calling over the waitress, so when he said, "Hello, miss" to the waitress,

Christina looked up because she thought he was talking to her. Garçon did that on purpose to gauge Christina's awareness.

"Miss, I will have a whiskey on the rocks and an order of fries. Thank you," Garçon said to the waitress.

"Anything for your girlfriend?" asked the waitress.

"She isn't my girlfriend. She is way too ugly to be my girlfriend," replied Garçon.

The waitress could not tell if he was serious or if he was playing, so she asked Christina, "Would you like anything? I am sure this gentleman would pay for it."

Christina replied, "No, thank you."

Now that he had Christina's attention, he said, "How dare you?"

"How dare I what?" asked Christina with intrigue.

"You are obviously mourning some kind of loss or heartbreak. How dare you come in here to do that?" asked Garçon.

"Excuses me, sir?" replied Christina in an annoyed manner.

"Before we get into this, what is your name?" asked Garçon.

"My name is Christina"

"Is that a German accent I hear?" asked Garçon.

"Yes, it is. Is there a problem?"

"No, I just figured that not only do I have to deal with the heartbreak another man is causing but also I will have to endure the fact that my love for you will be forbidden," said Garçon.

"Is that so?"

"It is. You have heartbreak written all over you. Plus, it's written in the European bylaws that the French and Germans can never be married."

Christina laughed at Garçon's joke about the French and Germans never being able to be married and responded, "Well, you are in luck. I am not in a loving mood today, and with that said, I think you should stay away, because I would eat your heart for dinner. Not because I want to, but because that is what we girls do when we are on the rebound."

Garçon could see her confidence and could tell she meant every bit of what she was saying. "Well, I am just happy I've gotten this far. I saw the carnage you have been leaving throughout this place. Nothing but the skulls and bones of all the men who have tried to come up to you. Which brings me to my point: why mourn here? Why give these men the hope that your being here alone means you are open to being theirs for either a night or an eternity? It's rather selfish if you ask me."

As Christina thought of her response, she had a devilish grin on her face. She replied, "Places like this help me figure out if my relationship is worth it. But I like you…" Christina waited for Garçon to finish her sentence by giving her his name.

"Just call me 1-A," said Garçon.

"Why choose that name?" she asked.

"Because I feel like that is where I'll be in your life. Not quite number one, but far from number two."

"OK, One-a. You've got it," she replied.

That wasn't what Garçon wanted to hear. He was usually able to get any woman that he wanted, and when Christina didn't correct him immediately, it made him want her more.

As his reflection of the night they met came to an end, Garçon began to regret walking over to her that day. The memories of that night were as fresh to him as the meeting he had this morning. The scenery outside his guarded motorcade did nothing to help get his mind off of her. He went deeper into his thoughts and began to plot out ways to get rid of her husband. The task wouldn't be easy, since he was a very powerful man, and that angered Garçon more. Throughout his entire time with Christina, all Garçon did was attempt to better himself so she would regret not choosing to be with him and instead staying with a man who was just as powerful as he was.

He couldn't even stay angry at her for long before his emotions turned to being upset with himself for allowing her to get that close to his heart and him not being able to move on. But his anger didn't stop there. The more he thought of today's meeting, the more he realized he had wasted his life chasing her. Now the end of society was coming, and he still had to play the Game of Thrones. He laughed out loud in the car as he thought that phrase.

"What is so funny, sir? Did you see something?" asked his assistant seated next to him.

"No. I am just laughing at a phrase my mates and I used to say when we were playing for the national team," responded Garçon.

"Oh really, and what phrase is that?" his assistant asked.

"The phrase is *the Game of Thrones*," said Garçon.

"You mean that old TV show?"

"Yes."

"Oh man, I loved that show! I used to watch it with my dad."

"Oh man, I really am getting old."

"Well, sir, what does the phrase mean?" asked the assistant.

"It means doing whatever it takes to win the seven kingdoms. For the participants, there are no rules, only results," responded Garçon.

"That must've originated from two men fighting over a prize. I am assuming the seven kingdoms represents whatever your goal is whether it's a woman, job or anything a man would aspire to attain. But, I think it represents a woman the majority of the time," she stated.

"That is quite perceptive. Just curious, how did you come up with that?"

"Instinctively, men have honor and a conscience about everything except when it comes to women. You guys will do anything to get the chance to sleep with a woman. I mean, we women get that, but we don't truly understand it because we see our vagina every day, so subconsciously we think, 'How anyone can fight over this ugly thing?' That's why we judge you guys for sleeping with multiple women. Not because we don't sort of understand it, but because we don't understand why you guys can't resist something so ugly and wrinkled. I understand this primal need to destroy everything in your path; I find it sexy actually. But I also respect that I can use that urge for all the free dinners I get."

Garçon was impressed with her response. She explained his phrase like no other person could, and he replied by saying, "If only you were older."

That remark left her with a smile because she knew Garçon would never cross the line.

The day was drawing to a close, and all Garçon could think about was Christina and how he wanted her to call him. But why would she? She only had an obligation to another man who wasn't even the right match for her. No matter what Garçon did, she was never going to leave her husband. For years he had wondered how his life would be if she did leave her husband.

As he stared out the window watching cars pass by, he saw a woman who resembled his love, and he quickly turned around as if he saw a ghost.

His sudden gesture made his guards jumpy.

"Is everything OK, sir?" one of the guards asked.

"Yes, all is well," Garçon replied.

He began to smile to himself, as he noticed his assistant looking at him nervously. Once their eyes met, he immediately pictured Christina's face on his assistant's body. The image overwhelmed his thought processes so much that it transported him to the last time they were together.

All he was able to think about that day was how nervous he was to see her. She had told him that she would be able to see him for about four hours because her husband was in France for an economic summit to discuss ways to secure the viability of the euro. The summit was tremendously important to France, and Garçon was required to be there, but he would not be able to see Christina for months if he did not take this chance to see her now. The decision to be late weighed on his mind so strongly that he nearly told her that he couldn't make it. He began to open and close the box to the black-and-white diamond earrings he had bought her, each time thinking of a different memory he shared with her in his arms.

The shine from the diamonds glazed in his eyes as if they were speaking to him. Each one was telling him that he should see her and that the only care in the world he should have was her. Each diamond longing to be in her ears, begging for him to put them there. They shined so brightly in the light that he began to daydream about how her face would glow with approval once she saw them. Her smile would be so bright, he would realize how being late was worth it. At that very moment, Garçon decided to forget the world around him and see the love of his life.

Because of his profile and the French media being so aggressive with watching his every step, seeing Christina was always very difficult. Little did the world know that years before, when a French hotel was being built by a developer he used to play soccer with, Garçon had instructed his friend to set up four rooms that were never to be rented out under any circumstances as well as an underground passage that only three people had access to. His inspiration for this was the Waldorf Astoria in New York City. The passage connected his presidential office directly to the hotel, so he could travel on his own without being seen.

The passage had six security doors that required a retina scan and fingerprint approval before they could be opened. On the right side of each door was a weapon and gas dispensers just in case enemies followed him in order to kidnap him. The gas was a powerful sleep agent that when inhaled would knock someone out immediately. No one in his cabinet or the outside world ever knew he had left his office unless he said so. Once he reached the hotel, a single elevator would wait for him that was directly connected to the rooms.

This particular elevator and the pathway leading to it were not on the hotel's building plans or listed in the French building plans office. They were only known by Garçon and his former soccer teammate. The workers used to use the elevator as a freight elevator during the hotel's construction, but it was closed down and hidden behind a wall once the hotel was completed. The elevator led to two different rooms on the fifty-sixth and fifty-seventh floors. The rooms connected to the elevator and were also adjoined to the two rooms directly above and below them. The room on the fifty-seventh floor was connected to a room on the fifty-eighth, and the room on the fifty-sixth floor was connected to a room on the fifty-fifth.

Whenever Christina came to town, she would stay at the hotel and reserve the room on the fifty-fifth floor. A fingerprint and retinal scanner located behind the refrigerator there activated a lift in the ceiling that came down to take her to the room above.

When Garçon entered the hotel room that day, she did not hear him, and his presence startled her. She was coming out of the shower, and she jumped up so quickly that her towel nearly fell to the floor as both of her hands went up to cover her face as she screamed. They both began to laugh.

"Luckily the rooms are soundproof, or we would be in trouble."

"Shouldn't you be there?" She pointed to the TV where a news reporter was reporting on the economic summit.

"I can't stay long, but I couldn't resist seeing you. I hate this power you have over me. One day I am going to get over you and find a woman who is going to make a man out of me."

As he said that, she walked over to him in a seductive manner and started to pull him toward her. "You can't leave me! You are mine. Besides, you need to stop talking. We have things to do, and you don't have a lot of time."

Her confidence was intoxicating to Garçon. She knew she had him, and there was nothing he could do about it. He had dedicated his whole life to doing whatever he could to impress her, but nothing worked. He was just her plaything. Their affair had been going on for years, and no matter how hard he tried to forget about her, it was impossible. He lived his life with no wife or kids just so she would be his first, even though she told him she would never give that to him.

Once he stopped reflecting and looked away from her eyes, he replied, "I guess you are right. As far as me being there," he pointed at the TV. "What is the point of being the leader of France if I can't be a little late? Besides, love is more important, and if that means rearranging my schedule, so I could see you and give you these—" Garçon took out the earrings and handed them to her, "then a man has to do what a man has to do."

Her face lit up with amazement when she opened the box. Garçon saw how happy she was. The smile she gave, made him smile from ear to ear and made it all seem worth it. He had waited months to see that face and was aroused immediately. Even in his daydreams of her face once she got the earrings, he did not expect what he got.

Garçon then tried to take off Christina's towel, but she said, "Stop. I want to put them on."

She left and went into the bathroom. Garçon started to get undressed in anticipation that she would be ready for him. But when she came out, it was not what he was expecting. Not only did she have the earrings on, but she had put on thigh-high fishnet stockings. Garçon had tried to get her to wear them for him for as long as he could remember. She would always forget them, or he wouldn't let her get a chance to put them on because he would attack her as soon as he saw her, but not this time. This time she took it upon herself to make sure she gave Garçon what he wanted.

Seeing her at the threshold of the door like that, Garçon became more aroused. He grabbed her hand and pulled her onto the bed with him. Fishnets drove him absolutely crazy, and the sight of her in them was absolutely one of the best visuals Garçon had ever seen.

But when he pulled her close, she resisted him by pulling her arm away.

"Don't grab me like I am yours because I am not," she said.

When she said that, it made Garçon absolutely furious, but that was her intention. She wanted Garçon to get angry because she wanted to be manhandled when he finally took her.

"I don't know why I even put up with you. My husband is a real man. Why do you think I would ever leave him for you?" she said as she broke loose from his grip.

"Look at how easy that was," she said, referring to pulling her arm away from him and walking to the other side of the room. She sat down in a chair and lit a cigarette.

Garçon got up from the bed and chased after her to the other side of the room. He did not realize that she was role-playing, and his rage was uncontrollable.

"Why are you saying these things to me?" he said with intense anger and passion.

Christina acted as if she didn't care and rolled her eyes. Garçon then pulled her off the chair and bent her down with her backside facing him and her face pinned up against the back of the chair.

"Why are you talking to me like this?" he asked again.

She took a drag of the cigarette and blew the smoke in his face.

Throughout Garçon's life, he was able to always please a woman sexually, but today his anger didn't allow him to think clearly, so he reverted to his primal nature and pulled her legs open and started to bite the back of her neck like a lion does when it mates. She pretended to try to turn around so she could push Garçon away, but that was not going to work, because the more she moved, the stiffer Garçon got. Although, this was all a part of Christina's plan and despite Garçon knowing Christina still wanted him, he decided to go along with her role-playing despite his feelings of overwhelming rage. She wanted to be dominated that day, and she knew how to manipulate Garçon's feelings in order to get him to do what she wanted.

Garçon was notorious for taking a long time to ejaculate, but once he turned her around and took in the sight of her body with the earrings on and the fishnets, he was unable to control himself. The orgasm he experienced was nothing like he had ever experienced before.

Garçon was a pleaser, so when he realized that she did not have an orgasm, he felt defeated. Then, all of a sudden, Christina began to cry. This immediately put Garçon on alert. All he could think about was Christina regretting seeing him because he had left her unsatisfied, but that was the furthest thing from her mind.

"My husband is a lying bastard!" she wept.

"What happened?"

"I always knew he was a cheating asshole, but when you are married to the chancellor of Germany, cheating becomes a part of life. But to cheat on me with a man! That is unforgivable!" cried Christina.

"Merchant is cheating on you with a man? Are you serious?" responded Garçon.

"Yes, a man. Fucking Fehrenbach, his ambassador to Morocco who lives in Safi. He's associated with his agency and is a ship captain who used to sail celebrities around the world."

Garçon was torn between staying to comfort her and encouraging her to leave Merchant and be with him or leaving right away for the summit where he was supposed to meet Merchant face-to-face, but he froze.

"Can you stay until this summit is over?" asked Garçon.

"You know I can't, but you have to get going. We will talk later."

Christina walked away from him and closed the bathroom door as Garçon just stared at the wall, speechless.

Suddenly he snapped him out of the vision of Christina's head on his assistant's body. That moment in the hotel room was one of the most regrettable experiences of his life until today in the meeting, when he let his emotions destroy the trust that Christina built with him.

At that very moment, the car stopped. One of his security detail opened the door. A bystander took a picture of President Garçon still sitting in the car and uploaded the picture to Instagram, and where he was tagged.

Abigail Bennett

As she looked at President Garçon's face on the Instagram site, Abigail Bennett reminisced about his fight with Chancellor Merchant and couldn't help but think how even more handsome he was in person. Today was the third time she had met him, but as handsome as she thought he was, she wasn't attracted to him. Bennett was the first unmarried prime minister of Canada, and, like Garçon, she was always criticized for it. But much like the men in that room, she had a secret that she never wanted the world to know. The reason she wasn't married was because she was only attracted to Black men and she was never able to overcome what people would think of her if she decided to marry one. As beautiful and rich as Bennett was, every man of power in Canada wanted to be with her. But powerful people only want what they cannot have, and having a powerful White man was available to her at the snap of a finger. What made her look at Garçon for so long was that he reminded her of her best friend's grandfather, former President Barack Obama.

The daughter of real estate tycoon Lucas Bennett, Bennett grew up with privilege but never allowed her legacy to dictate her path. During the Obama administration, race relations in the

United States had taken a turn for the worse. Once Obama left office, race wars over police killing Black males and not going to jail or facing any charges became a common occurrence. During that time, the largest northern migration of African Americans to Canada since the conclusion of the Civil War had commenced. One of the families that left the states was Sasha Obama's family, including her daughter, Jessica. Because her grandfather was the president, Jessica had the finances that allowed her to go to the same schools as Bennett, and they became friends. When his schedule allowed him and before his assassination during a rally to ease racial tension in America, Obama would visit his granddaughter. Bennett had met him on several occasions.

She remembered how tall and charismatic Obama was, and she loved how he would embrace her with a hug and kiss every time he saw her. He had a way of making her feel as if they had known each other forever. He was her first little girl crush.

One day she decided to talk to her grandmother about her feelings for Obama and why for some reason she was attracted to Black men. Her grandmother, widowed for many years, looked at Bennett and smiled and told her that she too had a secret.

Bennett's grandmother reflected on how she would tell her husband she was taking Bennett, who was a toddler at the time, out for a walk, but she would meet up with a man every time. That man was her grandmother's Black business partner, and she had been having an affair with him for over twenty years. On that day, her grandmother told Bennett that she had seen her kissing him while she was a baby; over time Bennett must have subconsciously developed that same attraction to Black men that her grandmother had.

That day Bennett's grandmother also told her of their family's history during the years of slavery in the United States and how her ancestors were responsible for housing slaves who escaped from America once they arrived in Canada. The Bennett family was responsible for helping over one hundred African American families create businesses in Canada during the 1800s. Those businesses acted as secret franchises for Bennett family corporations, which were insurance and exportation. All the African American families that the Bennett family helped to escape went to her family's business for insurance as well as exportation of their products to other regions of the world.

The outside world was unaware of the arrangements those Black-owned businesses had with the Bennett family, and with White faces used as fronts for the Black businesses, the money flowed in. They created a community within itself that prospered until desegregation hit America. Once that occurred, many of the Black businesses moved back to America because they thought that society had changed. By the time migration back to America was complete, the Bennett family business was beyond wealthy and was one of the largest financial services firm in the world.

As her grandmother reflected on the story, she began to laugh to herself.

"Why are you laughing, Grandma?" Bennett asked.

Her grandmother replied, "Because I think I did to you what my grandmother did to me. She created this attraction toward Black men with her interaction with them."

That very day Bennett made it her business to understand why so many Blacks were once again leaving America for Canada. During her research, she learned that much like the conditions in the 1800s, with modified voting laws, racism, and increasing police brutality, African Americans were being forced to migrate because they no longer felt safe in America. This resulted in middle- to upper-middle-class Blacks becoming the driving force of Canada's small-business economy.

Once Bennett graduated from college, she realized that the children of those individuals either had dual citizenship or were able to enter the United States freely based on the NATO treaty implemented by the Clinton administration. With cities such as Detroit and Atlantic City going under, Bennett began to organize a small group of Blacks to purchase property and create businesses in these blighted cities. The cities were large enough to house large numbers of African Americans, and the property was cheap enough to buy, so the new residents took pride in their communities.

But Bennett's plan didn't stop there. She began to develop political strategies to vote out the old politicians, which resulted in the police force and judgeships being changed to predominantly African American leadership. Whites who were in these cities were only allowed in prominent political positions if they fit two conditions. The individuals had to have either joined Black Greek letter organizations in college or be married to someone of the opposite race.

Bennett implemented these policies to ensure the politicians were progressive enough to understand the racism that affected the individuals they would be judging or representing in government. Once these processes were in place, Bennett ran for a city council seat in Montreal and used the office to organize dozens of Black-owned businesses in Detroit and Atlantic City. She convinced her father, who was CEO of her family's company, to back these businesses and purchase the abandoned casinos in both cities and turn them into office and residential space. The company received 35 percent of all revenue from the recruited companies with Bennett receiving 10 percent of all revenues, and the corporation receiving the other 25 percent.

She sold him on the idea of holding American property and political power in the same manner the Chinese began to in the early 1990s. Once the investments were made, the cities began to flourish, and all the remaining revenue never left them. The employees worked at the jobs. Once they were paid, they paid their mortgages to the community banks that gave those loans, and with all their living requirements being met within the cities, every business flourished.

Bennett spearheaded a program called Atlantic City Currency and Detroit Dollars, which was only available to residents of those cities. The program developed a directory of corporations, with the participating companies paying a fee to be listed in the directory. For every real US dollar exchanged, a person would get $1.50 to spend on any business listed in the directory. The incentive created a bond between the residents and the businesses within the cities. Once word got out, every educated Black person with a business wanted to move into Atlantic City or Detroit.

The Bennett Corporation organized the businesses to limit inclusion to the cities in order to maintain demand. Limiting inclusion worked perfectly because the residents that rebuilt the communities wanted to maintain the cities, and the newer residents would use their admission into these cities as a symbol of social status. In as little as fifteen years, the mind-set began to be that you weren't really Black if you didn't live in Detroit or Atlantic City. If a company outside of these cities had a Black applicant for an open position, the human resources representative would question if he or she really wanted to work there or just wanted to stay long enough to build up a résumé to be admitted to those cities on a later date. This forced rejected Blacks to mirror these cities in other abandoned locations such as Flint, Michigan, and Wichita, Kansas, or to settle underdeveloped cities in rural areas.

Over time, America began to suffer economically because the penal system had fewer Blacks, which affected all branches of government. Through Bennett's strategy, both cities created a culture of elite Blacks in America, and the world took notice. Once the time came, she decided to run for mayor of Montreal. No one ever knew she was the brains behind the efforts in America, but every prominent African American endorsed her candidacy based on Detroit and Atlantic City's influence.

But there was also a dark side to the Bennett Corporation's backing. Although their assistance with those communities was based on good intentions, the locations they selected were very strategic. With Detroit and Atlantic City being on the water and the judges as well as the police forces firmly behind the community, the Bennett Corporation used this as a prime opportunity to import drugs into those cities.

With marijuana being sold illegally throughout the United States due to federal mandates overturning state laws allowing weed to be sold, it was getting harder and harder for weed smokers to experience the same highs they once had, and that's where the Bennett Corporation saw a business opportunity. With none of the citizens in those cities using drugs, the sales went to primarily rural White communities, which no one had a problem with.

The business owners of the cities let the drugs pass through because they wanted those communities to feel the same effects of drugs that the Black communities had felt during the 1960s through the 1990s as well as because they were loyal to the Bennett Corporation. But many of them were also God-fearing Christians, so their consciences were in complete conflict with allowing the illegal imports to continue. Similar to CVS stores stopping the sale of cigarettes in 2014, the Bennett Corporation negotiated a time frame with both cities to cease the drug operation within a year if both cities were able to come up with legitimate businesses that would replace the income lost from the drug sales.

The drug imports were so lucrative that any business would have to be substantial in order to fulfill this criterion. The truth was, Bennett didn't expect the leadership of either city to come up with an idea that would replace the drug revenue, but that was the point. She just wanted them to feel as though they had a choice in the matter.

With gun laws being relaxed throughout the nation, Detroit business owners began to buy out all the gun companies under shell corporations with White CEOs that had pledged Black fraternities and sororities in college. Once all the American gun companies were purchased, they began to sell guns that could be operated only with access codes.

White politicians were lobbied by these gun companies to pass legislation that only allowed guns with access codes to be sold in America. The passage of the new laws went through after Senator Joseph Locket's daughter was accidently shot by her brother while playing with a firearm owned by the family. Had the gun only been fired when the required access code was entered, his daughter would be alive.

The law passed through both the Senate and Congressional Houses with ease out of fear for child safety. Once the law swept through both houses, Detroit came up with a device called TALK. TALK could be worn around the neck of someone who did not have a criminal record and was under the age of twelve. The device would not allow any gun to be fired if the gun was pointed in the direction of a child wearing this device. A hologram would emerge from the gun telling the shooter that the gun would not be able to be fired and that before he or she pulled the trigger, the parties involved should talk.

Every parent in America purchased the device under the assumption it was protecting the children. The companies marketed the device in the same manner as immunizations. Yet there was an intentional flaw in the device. The batteries had to be replaced every six months, and a service fee for the program had to be paid on an annual basis. This was done to make sure the Bennett Corporation would continue to receive a profit, so there would be no reason to maintain the drug trade in secret. Once the US market was monopolized, Detroit began to sell the technology to other countries with gun laws similar to those of the United States.

Atlantic City developed medical technology that would allow humans to grow limbs back and heal, much the same way octopuses do. Atlantic City didn't want to have this technology in the world because they were eager for all the racist and sick people of the world to die off. Once the technology was mastered, Atlantic City sold it to the highest bidder, because the insurance companies did not want this technology available since it would cost them billions of dollars in revenue.

But little did the Bennett Corporation know that Atlantic City had no intention of developing a device with long-lasting profit margins because the city's motivation was only to buy them ten years of time to develop the next invention. This measure was implemented to ensure constant innovation within the city.

Once the sale was completed, the city gave over its portion of the earnings to the Bennett Corporation, and that ended all drug imports within Atlantic City. Leadership in both cities knew that wouldn't stop the Bennett Corporation from its practice, but they did not care since it was not going on in their cities.

Soon after her family's company became one of the richest corporations in the world, Bennett decided to run for Prime Minister of Canada. The funds for her campaign were so massive that she won by a landslide.

But after the meeting today, Bennett knew that with the rules of this "new earth," the cities she had helped rebuild, Detroit and Atlantic City, could be affected by the men in that room. But she was able to rest assured that those communities were advanced enough to pass the testing that would be placed before them. Bennett's hope was that the men she secretly desired would still be around once the final numbers were tallied. But if not, she would not have any problem with hiding a couple, just as her ancestors did during slavery.

The Next Day

"Sir, I will not disappoint you today?" stated Johnson nervously.

"You almost cost us this entire operation! Your posturing was unnecessary and nearly wasted our efforts to have this meeting. Killing Vice President Perez was the only way we could get all of these leaders here without alerting the world of this situation and your tactics nearly squandered this opportunity." responded a silver haired man on Johnson's monitor in an extremely angry tone.

"He is absolutely right, Johnson. There is only one reason we chose Perez for assassination rather than you. We couldn't risk Perez changing his mind about this plan once our campaign for Central and South America are ready and the war has concluded and the earth is back on its orbital path." stated an African American woman.

There was one more individual of Middle Eastern decent on the video conference that was just observing the call and not responding because his colleagues were telling Johnson everything he was thinking. He then stated, "You know what to do. Be professional and show sympathy. Introduce Connor and give them their instructions and nothing more because I fear what is going to happen now based on your insensitivity towards this situation."

"I understand and I will not let any of you down."

Johnson felt ashamed and ended the video conference with the three individuals. When the group entered the room, Johnson was already there. There would be no grand standing or coming late to make an entrance this time. Johnson was ready for business, but to his surprise, the other leaders came into the room with an aura of acceptance. Each knew his or her role and was ready to be a part of the bigger picture to save the world because there was only one to save. Johnson thought he would have to convince one or two of them further about the plan, but that was not necessary.

"Fellow leaders, meet Connor Mathews. He will be leading the legislative changes in the United States once the war commences. Most of you may remember him as my political foe, but in this fight we are on the same side. In your folder, you will find his profile and all the information you need to know about him," said Johnson.

The room looked at Mathews. By the looks on their faces, Johnson could tell that they already trusted everything about him, and that was why Johnson had picked him. Connor had a look to him that made people love him immediately. The look was so genuine that Johnson often wondered how he had beat Mathews for the oval office in the first place, but that was the past. This was about the future, and it was time for Mathews to do what was right for his family, his country, and the future of the world.

Once the introduction was complete, Russian President Alexandrov stood up and said, "Welcome Mr. Mathews. Now, Mr. President, on behalf of the members in this room, I would like for you to know, we are ready for war." He reached into his jacket pocket and pulled out what looked like a thick pen with a glowing red button on the top and pushed it. Johnson was not sure what to make of this as he and Alexandrov stared eye to eye. The stare only lasted for seconds, but to both of them it seemed like it could have gone on for an hour and then a loud boom occurred that shook the room.

The members of the room looked out of the window to see what happened and as they looked to the east, each of them saw fire and smoke coming from the direction of the White House. With the entire room rushing towards the window for a closer look, Johnson realized that Alexandrov was still seated in his chair as if he expected this to happen. Johnson looked back towards the explosion in such fear that when he turned around to confront Alexandrov his hand left an imprint on the window.

"What did you do?" screamed Johnson.

"I just let you know, that America isn't the only country with weapons."

As Johnson and Alexandrov continued to stare at each other, the security details for all of the members rushed in to evacuate the leaders from the room when all of a sudden Yo screamed at the top of his lungs, "WAR!"

54106084R00122

Made in the USA
Charleston, SC
23 March 2016